"Cider?"

She lifted her mug for show, but he put his hand over hers and guided her drink to his mouth. "It's hot," she whispered.

"Mmm." He pressed his lips together. "I'll pass."

"Would you like something else?" she offered, and he shook his head. "You're welcome to stay through the holidays. A week was your bet, not mine."

"Maybe I was hopin' you'd raise me." She gave him a quizzical look. "Try it," he challenged, his eyes mesmerizing her. "Aren't you curious?"

"What would happen?"

"That's not the way the game is played. You gotta say, I'll see your week—" he lifted his hand slowly toward her hair, moved a barely visible strand with a barely moving finger "—and raise you all the way into the next."

"I can't afford you . . ." She couldn't move. His cool finger touched her cheek, trailed tingles to her chin. "…that…long." His kiss was impossibly tender. A touch of warm breath, a taste of spice.

An all-knowing smile. "Yeah, you can."

Dear Reader,

I'm back, just as I promised in my letter to you in *In Care of Sam Beaudry*. This time it's the special holiday delivery from Silhouette Special Edition of a special cowboy—Sam's brother, Zach Beaudry.

Oh, I do love me some cowboys. One in the flesh and numerous on paper. I married the former, and the rest is history. (Not to mention her story.) I met Clyde Eagle on June 8 in the year…well, in the past century. But I remember it as though it happened last week. He was dressed in a red Western-style shirt, scuffed boots, a straw cowboy hat…and let's just say he wore his Wranglers as only a cowboy can. And—icing on the cake—he was gentling a young buckskin horse. This prim Eastern college girl made a photographic memory that day that would make its mark on every romantic tale she's written from that century to this.

Zach Beaudry is one of those paper cowboys, but with my creativity and your imagination, we're about to bring him to life. Zach's a professional bull rider who's almost forgotten what *home* means. He's tired, broke and half-frozen when he lands on the doorstep of the Double D Ranch, and he's risked every part of his body except his heart. But Ann Drexler is about to remedy that little oversight.

Welcome to the Double D Wild Horse Sanctuary. *One Cowboy, One Christmas* is only the beginning.

Happy holidays!

Kathleen Eagle

KATHLEEN EAGLE

ONE COWBOY,
One Christmas

♥ *Silhouette*®

SPECIAL EDITION®

Published by Silhouette Books

America's Publisher of Contemporary Romance

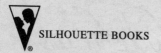

SILHOUETTE BOOKS

ISBN-13: 978-0-373-65493-2

ONE COWBOY, ONE CHRISTMAS

Recycling programs for this product may not exist in your area.

Visit Silhouette Books at www.eHarlequin.com

Printed in U.S.A.

KATHLEEN EAGLE

published her first book, a Romance Writers of America Golden Heart Award winner, with Silhouette Books in 1984. Since then she has published more than forty books, including historical and contemporary, series and single-title, earning her nearly every award in the industry. Her books have consistently appeared on regional and national bestseller lists, including the *USA TODAY* list and the *New York Times* extended bestseller list.

Kathleen lives in Minnesota with her husband, who is Lakota Sioux. They have three grown children and three lively grandchildren.

For Mary Bracho
extraordinary teacher, cherished friend

Chapter One

"Don't die on me, Zel."

I've been dying, Zachary. I've been trying to tell you that.

"Come on, Zel. You know how much I love you, girl. You're all I've got. Don't do this to me here. Not *now*."

But it had to be here because it would be now. His beloved pickup truck, Zelda, had quit on him, and Zach Beaudry had no one to blame but himself. He'd taken his sweet time hitting the road, and then miscalculated a shortcut. For all he knew he was a hundred miles from gas. But even if they were sitting next to a pump, the three dollars he had in his pocket wouldn't get him out of South Dakota, which was not where he wanted to be right now.

Not even reliable old Zelda could get him much of anywhere on fumes. He was sitting out in the cold in the middle of nowhere. And getting colder. Zach made no apologies to anyone for being a fair-weather lover.

Cowboy. Fair-weather cowboy. As a lover, he was the all-weather model.

He shifted the pickup into Neutral and pulled hard on the steering wheel, using the downhill slope to get her off the blacktop and into the roadside grass, where she shuddered to a standstill. He stroked the padded dash. "You'll be safe here."

But Zach would not. It was getting dark, and it was already too damn cold for his cowboy ass. Was it December yet? November in this part of the country was hard enough on beat-up bones and worn-out joints. Zach's battered body was a barometer, and he was feeling South Dakota, big-time. He'd have given his right arm to be climbing into a hotel hot tub instead of a brutal blast of north wind. The right was his free arm anyway. Damn thing had lost altitude, touched some part of the bull and caused him a scoreless ride last time out. Whole lotta pain for an ugly little goose egg.

It wasn't scoring him a ride this night, either. A carload of teenagers whizzed by, topping off the insult by laying on the horn as they passed him. It was at least twenty minutes before another vehicle came along. He stepped out and waved both arms this time, damn near getting himself killed. Whatever happened to *do unto others?* In places like this, decent people didn't leave each other stranded in the cold.

His face was feeling stiff, and he figured he'd better start walking before his toes went numb. He struck out for a distant yard light, which was the only sign of human habitation in sight. He couldn't tell how distant, but he knew he'd be hurting by the time he got there, and he was counting on some kindly old man to be answering the door. No shame among the lame.

It wasn't like Zach was fresh off the operating table—it had been a few months since his last round of repairs—but he hadn't given himself enough time. He'd lopped a couple of weeks off the near end of the doc's estimated recovery time, rigged up a brace, done some heavy-duty taping and climbed onto another bull. Hung in there for five seconds—four seconds past feeling the pop in his hip and three seconds short of the buzzer.

He could still feel the pain shooting down his leg with every step. Only this time he had to pick the damn thing up, swing it forward and drop it down again on his own. Couldn't even wangle a ride off his own kind.

Pride be damned, he just hoped *somebody* would be answering the door at the end of the road. The light in the front window was a good sign.

The four steps to the covered porch might as well have been four hundred, and he was looking to climb them with a lead weight chained to his left leg. His eyes were just as screwed up as his hip. Big black spots danced around with tiny red flashers, and he couldn't tell what was real and what wasn't. He stumbled over some shrubbery, steadied himself on the porch railing and peered between vertical slats.

There in the front window stood a spruce tree with a silver star affixed to the top. Zach was pretty sure the red sparks were all in his head, but the white lights twinkling by the hundreds throughout the huge tree, those were real. He wasn't too sure about the woman hanging the shiny balls. Most of her hair was caught up on her head and fastened in a curly clump, but the light captured by the escaped bits crowned her with a golden halo. Her face was a soft shadow, her body a willowy silhouette beneath a long white gown. If this was where the mind ran off to when cold started shutting down the rest of the body, then Zach's final worldly thought was, *This ain't such a bad way to go.*

He wanted to tell her, touch her, thank her. If she would just turn to the window, he could die looking into the eyes of a Christmas angel. She would find him, know him, forgive and love him, all in a look, and he would go to his Maker feeling good inside. Fighting to free his leg from a dried-out bush, he stumbled over a stone face with the bulging eyes, fangs and flaring nostrils of a hideous watchdog sitting on the porch beside the steps. It took all the strength he had left to throw the hellhound off him. Down the steps he went.

But he went down fighting.

"Sally?"

Something—*someone*—had fallen. The glass ornament that had just slipped from Ann's fingers crunched under her slippered foot.

"Sally, what happened?"

No answer. No movement in the foyer. She would have heard the door if her sister had tried to sneak outside. Ann flipped the porch light on and peered through the narrow window flanking the front door. One of her gargoyles lay in pieces at the edge of the porch. Ann's heartbeat tripped into overdrive as she opened the door, expecting the worst. "Sally?"

"What's going on?" Sally called out from down the hall.

She was safe inside, thank God. If Ann knew her older sister, Sally had had her fingers crossed when she'd promised not to leave the house anymore without telling somebody where she was going. Sally hated being treated like an invalid, and Ann tried not to do it. They seldom talked about Sally's condition, especially when the symptoms were in remission. They knew the pain of multiple sclerosis, each in her own way. It had become a third sister. The cruel and unpredictable one.

"I don't know," Ann said. "Probably just the wind."

Or the fourteen-year-old she'd presented with an ultimatum at school earlier in the week. *If we can't depend on you to show up when you're supposed to, Kevin, we'll have to reassess the terms of our agreement.*

"It sounded like a battering ram. Where's that dog when you need him?"

"Someplace warm." And no doubt having a good laugh. The dog and the boy had become a team over the summer, which had been part of the plan. Kevin Thunder Shield needed a loyal and true friend, and Baby needed a boy of her own. Ann just never knew with Kevin. Maybe he'd gotten a ride and she'd go out to the barn and find clean stalls. Wouldn't that be a nice surprise? "My gargoyle's broken, but other than that…"

There was something on the top step. A glove? Ann grabbed her parka off the hefty hook under the hat rack and plunged her arm into the sleeve.

"Sounds like a trespasser with good taste," Sally said. "Maybe a wandering gnome."

"He left a clue," Ann reported as she opened the door. "Cover me. I'm going out there." It was an old joke between them, but it used to be Sally stepping out in front. The idea of little Annie serving as a convincing backup for her once-mighty sister was almost laughable.

But times and conditions had changed. Stepping out had become Ann's job, and what she found was hand in glove. Hand attached to arm attached to the rest of a man's body draped facedown over her front-porch steps.

"Oh…dear God."

"What is it, Annie?"

"Stay inside." For what it was worth, Ann tossed the order over her shoulder as she stepped onto the porch. "It's colder than…" Her nightclothes puddled around her thin slippers as she squatted close to the man's head. She clutched the front of her parka together with one hand and gingerly lifted the brim of his black cowboy hat with the other. "Hey. Mister. Are you…" *Oh. Dear. God. No. Way.*

"Who's out there, Annie?"

"Sally, please stay—"

Too late. Sally was standing in the doorway, leaning heavily on her cane. "Is he drunk?"

Ann leaned close to his face, took a sniff and shook her head. "He'd be better off if he were," she decided. "I think he's frozen."

"Totally?"

He answered with a groan.

"I know him." Sally suddenly had her sister's back. "That's—"

"Will you *please* get back in the house?" Ann knew him, too. Better than her sister did, she suspected, but it had been years. Eight and a half, to be about a month short of exact. "Hey." She touched his shoulder. "Hey, mister, can you stand up? Or maybe just…"

"That's Zach Beaudry," Sally said. "He's a bull rider. Used to be *really* good. I remember—"

The man groaned again and mumbled something about a pickup. Ann moved around to his side, down two steps, and tried to haul him up by his arm. Then by her two arms, an effort that nearly sent both of them down another two steps.

"Did something happen? Are you hurt?" His pile-lined denim jacket didn't look very warm, but it was clean. "I don't see any blood."

"He's frozen," Sally reminded her. "He must have walked from the road."

"I'll get you in the house, but you have to help me," Ann told the cowboy hat, and then she warned her sister, "Not you! I'll do it. You hold the door." She sat him up against the railing. "Can you grab on here, and I'll… That's it, that's it." He almost fell over on her before he got his legs underneath him—railing under one arm, Ann under the other. "Okay, two steps up." He managed one. "Now the left."

"Left side…no good."

"How about the right?"

"Solid."

"Okay, so…hang on." She moved around to his left side. "We'll figure out a way to get you to a doctor."

"Just thaw-awww…" He tried and failed to hold his own, took a moment to brace himself against her slim-shouldered buttress, and tried again. Through her parka and his jacket, Ann could feel the violent quiver in his left hip. The cause was more than mere cold. "…thaw me out. *Damn.*"

"I'm afraid you've broken something."

"Yeah." He waved his free arm toward the pottery shards scattered across the porch. "Hadda…kill that… dog. S-sorry."

"I'll put him in Grandma's room," Ann told her sister, the doorstop. "No way can we get him up the stairs."

Grandma had been dead for fifteen years, but the spare room in the back of the house was still Grandma's. Sally had the master bedroom on the main floor, and the hired man had his own bunkhouse, so Ann had the second floor all to herself. If nothing else, there was no shortage of sleeping quarters at the Double D Ranch.

"We should put him in some warm water first." Sally

closed the front door and ducked under Zach's free arm, where she'd been once before. Briefly. "Or tepid water. Can you handle yourself in the bathtub, Zach?"

"Handle my...self?"

"Get your blood circulating again," Sally chirped. She'd been hurting and tired an hour ago, but cowboys—on TV or, better yet, in person—never failed to put some lift in her voice, which was music to momentarily dispel all Ann's misgivings about the man. After so many years, why not?

"Hands f-frozen," the cowboy muttered. "Can't handle m-much."

"How about your clothes? Can you take your clothes—oops." Ann grabbed the newel post and redoubled her support. "Steady."

"Blackin' out a little."

He was leaning a lot. The hard brim of that big hat clobbered her in the eye. That hat. She remembered trying to find the windows to his soul in the shadows, but from where she had lain, he'd been all succulent lips, chiseled nose and hat brim.

Aren't you going to take off your hat?

That's up to you.

Ann grabbed his hat and scored a ringer over the newel post as they started down the hall. She kept her eyes on the road and off the passenger as the threesome bounced off the walls a few times on their way to the bathroom, where Sally used the rubber end of her cane to push the door wide open. She took the lead but stepped aside with a nod toward the toilet. "Sit down.

No, wait." Again the cane extended her reach, and the toilet lid clattered over the seat.

Their guest gave a dry chuckle. "Up for b-boys, down for girls. I'm a…"

"Here." While Sally started running the bathwater, Ann shouldered him into place over the toilet seat. *Heave*… "Sit right here, Zach."

"No, I'm good. Boys can go…" *ho* "…outside. But don't tell Ma." He looked up at Ann and frowned as she unbuttoned his long-on-style, lean-on-insulation jacket. "Ma?"

Sally grabbed her arm. "You'd better let me handle that, Annie."

"I don't think so. He's a big hunk of dead weight." His pathetic excuse for a laugh turned into a feeble groan. Ann closed her eyes and tugged on his belt buckle. "I just hope he's wearing some kind of underwear." Not that she was prudish, really.

Well, maybe a little.

"Me, too," he muttered.

"How's the water, Sally?" Ann straddled his leg and started working on a boot. "Help me out, Zach. Wiggle your foot a little."

"Can't feel 'em. Musta lost 'em."

"Just a little," she coaxed, and felt a little movement, a little slippage. "That's good."

"Aaaaa!"

"There. Found a foot."

"It sure smells like a foot," Sally said in response to the drop of a ripe black sock.

"Looks like a bunch of red peppers." Ann gently curled her hand around five stiff toes. Zach sucked air between his teeth, and she quivered deep in her stomach.

"I think red is good. You don't want to see any blueberries," Sally said, and he groaned again. "Or raisins. Or—"

"Not hungry." He slumped, and his forehead rested against Ann's hip. "Gimme a minute to get…"

Ann slipped her arm around his back. "Okay, let's get you in the tub."

"You have to get his jeans off, Annie."

"Well, we have to get him up."

"I…I can…" He floundered and swayed, but with a little help he stood for his undressing.

Ann drew a deep breath, unbuttoned, unzipped and unseated his jeans. Brief boxers answered the earlier question. They were gray and snug, and he was an innie.

Hands on her shoulders, he steadied himself and posed a new one. "Am I up?"

Sally had the nerve to laugh.

"Lift your leg," Ann ordered. He did, but he almost lost what little balance he'd achieved. "Not on me!"

"What kind of a dog—" flailing, he grabbed the side of the tub and stepped free of his jeans "—you take me for?"

"The kind that's better thawed." On hands and knees Ann bumped his leg with her shoulder. "Can you step in the tub, please? Use the rail."

She found herself looking up at her sister between

a pair of sparsely hairy legs. Sally was leaning heavily on her cane, but her grin was easily worth Ann's indignity.

"Rail?"

"Like you're getting down in the chute, Zach." Sally helped him find her safety rail. "Slow and—"

"Yeowww!"

"—easy," Sally warned as he went down like a drunk on a banana peel. His hold on the safety rail was all that kept him from going under.

Ann was soaked. "Trust me, it isn't hot."

Knees in the air, Zach slid down the back of the tub, up to his chin in rocking and rolling water. Ann reached for his shoulders and held him still. "Just for a few minutes."

His sporadic shivers shifted to steady shuddering.

"You have to rub to get the blood flowing," Sally instructed from the sidelines. "Unless there's frostbite. No rubbing frostbite."

"How will I know if something's frostbitten?"

"You start rubbing, it'll fall off in your hand."

"Don't…" Zach waved a trembling finger under Ann's nose.

"Annie won't get your gun, cowboy."

"Sally!"

"He's turning beet-red." Sally waved the end of her cane over the tub like a magic wand. "That's what I call a royal flush."

"Like hell," Zach grumbled as Ann pushed his hand into the water.

"No, really," Sally insisted.

"Yeah, really," he groaned as Ann kneaded gently, his big hand sandwiched in both of hers. "Hurts like hell."

"I'm telling you, red is good." Sally took a seat on the toilet. "Rub his feet, Annie. Go easy."

"I'm not sure about the rubbing." But she tended to his fingers, simply holding them between her palms, one hand at a time. He protested and then gave over. Or under. Or out. His breathing had slowed, as though he were drifting off to sleep. "I think we should call someone for advice, Sally. At least find out—"

"I'm good," he said. "I promise. No…no trouble."

"I'll Google it." Sally punctuated her decision with a thump of her cane. "Back in a few."

"Call Ask-A-Nurse." Ann preferred fresh brainpower to search-engine options. She spoke quietly to Zach. "If there's any chance I'm causing any damage or you feel like any of your parts might fall off, you will speak up, won't you?"

"Uh-uh," he muttered. "Startin' to feel better."

"I can have an ambulance here in—"

"Don't." He opened his eyes and galvanized her with a curious look.

Oh, God, don't let him remember me. Her insides buzzed, horror and hope bouncing off each other within the thin-skinned bottle that was Ann Drexler. *Dear God, let me be memorable.*

The question in his eyes dissolved, unspoken and unresolved. Or simply unimportant. "Please don't. I'll… be on my feet…"

She shook off the moment, turning her hands into an envelope for five long toes. "Can you feel your—"

"Yeah. Barely. Don't break 'em."

"Glass toes?" She smiled, half tempted to try giving them a tickle. They'd been molded into the shape of a cowboy boot. Naked, they were curled and cute. Flaming piggies.

"Yeah. Like the rest of me. Ice, maybe, but you…" He braced his hands on either side of his hips and struggled to gain control of his seat. "Ahh, you're an angel."

"Ice princess, according to the last guy I went out with."

"And sent packing," Sally put in as she parked her wheelchair in the doorway. "Brought you a ride, Zach. I call him Ferdinand. He won't buck, but he can spin."

"Lemme at 'im." Zach started up, sat back down, hung his head chin to chest. "Damn."

"Easy, cowboy." Ann sat back on her heels, watching her sister rise laboriously from her chair and worrying about how much the excitement had tired her out. But Sally was clearly pleased to take part in the rescue, and, as ever, her pleasure pleased Ann. "Okay, Zach, here comes the tricky part."

"The packing?"

So he'd caught that. Was this some kind of in-and-out game? Zach in, Zach out.

Private joke, public laugh.

"The getting you out and dry and dressed." Ann glanced up at Sally, who thought she was laughing *with* her. Little did she know. "Where's Hoolie when we need him?"

"There's a dance at the VFW tonight," Sally said.

"Damn." Zach's mantra.

"You aren't missing any—" Ann turned in time to get sloshed as he tried and failed to get up on his own. She laid her hand on his slick, sleek shoulder. "Slow down, Zach."

"Still just a little…" He reached for support and found Sally's safety rail on the one hand and Ann on the other.

She threaded her arm beneath his and around his back, braced herself and helped him haul himself out of the water. *Whoosh.* He was heavy, wet and slippery, but she wasn't going down under him. Not this time.

"Step over and out, Zach."

"Out-ssside," he muttered as he released the rail and piled a few more pounds on Ann's shoulders. "Jeez, I drew a spinner."

"Hang on. Sally? Towels."

"Right behind him, little sister." Sally wrapped a blue bath sheet around Zach's waist. "Got my wheels right outside the door, along with some chamomile tea. According to my Googling, we shouldn't be—"

"Be careful," Ann warned. "Wet floor." One slip, and they'd all go down like bowling pins.

They wrapped Zach like a mummy, sat him in Sally's wheelchair and swore to him he was not on his way to another hospital, nor hell, nor heaven, nor—for the moment—Texas.

Dressing him wasn't an option, so they helped him peel off his wet shorts and tucked him into bed like an overgrown baby while Sally ticked off a list of Internet pointers about hypothermia. "We need to warm him all over, inside and out. Going after fingers and toes first was a mistake, but oh, well."

Zach gave a shivery chuckle. "Oh, well."

"Prop him up so he can drink this."

Ann turned and scowled at the "Mustang Love" coffee mug decorated with a picture of a ponytailed girl and a high-tailed colt. "You prop him up."

Sally gave a smug smile. "No can do."

"*I'll* p-prop…" But he didn't move.

Ann countered with an irritated sigh, stuffed a second pillow under his shoulders, tucked her arm beneath his head and signaled her sister for a handoff. The soothing warmth of the mug settled her, and she calmly shared—warm tea, warm bed, warm heart. She was a Good Samaritan. Nothing more.

His dark, damp hair smelled like High Plains winter—fresh, pure and utterly unpredictable. She remembered the way it had fallen over his forehead the first time she'd taken off his hat, the way she'd turned him from studlike to coltish with a wave of her hand, the glint in his eyes gone a little shy, his smile sweet and playful. Remove the lid, let the heart light shine. Hard to believe she'd ever been that naive. Undone by a hunk of hair.

Deliberately she hadn't noticed this time. But she noticed it now. Nice hair.

"Maybe you should give him some skin, Annie."

Ann looked up. *Get real.*

"Full-body contact is the best human defrost system," Sally said with a shrug.

"Is this the gospel according to Google?"

"Well, it does make perfect—"

"I believe," Zach muttered.

Ann filled his mouth to overflowing with tea.

"From now on, when in South Dakota, remember the dress code," Sally said as she caught the dribble from the corner of his mouth with one of the towels he was no longer wearing. "Thermal skivvies after Halloween."

"'S why I'm headin'…for Texas."

"Not tonight," Sally said. "You been rode pretty hard."

"Thanks for not…p-puttin' me up wet." Eyes at half-mast he looked up at Ann and offered a wan smile. "S-sorry to b-bother you this t-time of n-night."

"Still cold?" She imagined crawling into bed with him, shook her head hard and tucked the comforter under his quivering chin. "We can still get you to the—"

"No way," he said. "I'm good." He turned his head and pressed his lips to her fingers. "You're an angel."

Hardly. Angels didn't quiver over an innocent kiss on the hand. They glided away looking supremely serene.

"Tree topper," he whispered. Hypothermia had given him a brain freeze. Maybe tomorrow he'd remember her.

And maybe she could learn to glide and look supremely serene.

Chapter Two

Waking up in a strange room was nothing new for Zach Beaudry, but waking up in a pretty room was pretty damn strange. His usual off-ramp motel—good for a thousand-of-a-kind room and a one-size-fits-all bed—suited him just fine. No fault, no foul, no pressure.

He closed his eyes. Purple. Everything around him was purple. Motels didn't do much purple. The color of pressure.

Where the hell was he? He felt like he'd been wasted for a week and had no clue what he'd started out celebrating. If he'd been drinking to forget, he'd accomplished his mission. He remembered bits and pieces—a long walk, a glittering Christmas tree, a pretty woman in white—but they didn't come together in a way that made a lot of sense. How had he landed in a bed—somebody's *personal* bed—surrounded by personal pictures of real people, furniture that wasn't bolted down, and colors only a woman could love?

His head pounded. The pressure was on. If he had to pay the piper, he was owed at least a fond memory of the song, not to mention the wine and the woman. Hell, for all he knew, *he* might owe *her*. Before she walked in, he needed to neutralize his disadvantage by recalling who she was, what she looked like, and whether it had been good for her.

But nothing was clicking for him except his badly abused joints. Jacking himself into a sitting position was a dizzying experience, and he was about ready to crawl back under the mostly purple covers when he heard female voices outside the door.

"...take him into the clinic this morning."

"Why? I checked on him. He's still breathing. His color is better."

"Even so…"

They sounded familiar, these voices. Familiar *to* him and *with* him. *Breathing? Check. Color? Approved.*

Even so?

"They don't like doctors, these guys. Doctors tell them all kinds of stuff they don't want to hear."

"Nobody wants to be told his toes might fall off."

Zach pulled the flowery quilt into his lap as he looked down at his dangling feet. He counted ten toes, all attached. In a minute he'd try moving them.

"Heard on the radio the temperature dropped more

than thirty degrees last night. Old-timers say the winter's gonna be one for the record books."

"They say that every fall."

"Sometimes they're right."

"All the times they were wrong didn't get recorded."

Zach smiled inside his head. His face wasn't ready. Cracking wasn't out of the question. But he was a cowboy, and like all dying breeds of men, he was particularly fond of old-timers. Kind women with soft voices gave him a good feeling, too, and the survivor in him was bent on rounding up all the good feelings he could find.

"If he isn't sick, he's probably hungry. Either way…"

A tentative fist knocked on the door.

"Both, but hungry's in the lead," Zach answered.

The door swung open, and an angel appeared.

Where had *that* come from? Zach had used some sappy lines in his life, but *angel* wasn't a word likely to leap off his tongue. Still, it fit. The mass of golden curls surrounded her doll's face like a halo, and she looked so slight in her crisp white top and slim jeans that he could picture her taking flight in the right kind of updraft.

"Oh!" She pinked up real pretty when she laid eyes on him. Doll face. He'd never say anything like that, either, but it sure fit. "You're up," she observed, considerably down the scale from her *oh!* "How…how are you feeling?"

"Dazed and clueless." He bunched up the quilt for better coverage below his waist. "Last I remember I was headed for Texas."

"You still have a long way to go, then."

"Ran outta gas." He glanced at a bright window with frilly see-through curtains, looking for a hint. Tree branches didn't cut it. "I'm pretty sure that's a corner piece to this whole puzzle."

"Hoolie says it's more than that, but the important thing is—"

Tree outside the window. *Tree inside the window.*

"Is it Christmas already?"

"We have almost a month yet." She glanced over her shoulder as she pushed the door wide. Back to him. "I think you should see a doctor. Do you need help getting dressed?"

"I need to know where I am."

"You're at the Double D Ranch in South Dakota, cowboy." Voice number two rolled in on a wheelchair. "Sally Drexler," she announced and then nodded toward the angel. "My sister, Ann."

"Drexler, the stock contractor? I remember the name."

"And I remember Zach Beaudry. I've been sidelined for quite a while now, but we've actually met before. Back when I was sassy and nimble."

"Hey, I hear you, Sally. Rodeo's a cruel mistress. One good kick in the nimble and all you've got left is sass." And his was kinda twisting naked in the wind here.

"That's the Zach Beaudry I remember," Sally said with a slightly off-balance smile. "You're a poet and you know it. Especially when those sports commentators come at you with a microphone."

"Not anymore. I don't like questions that begin with

how disappointing is it, and they generally don't like my answers." He turned to Angel Ann. "Now, your question was…"

"Do you want to see a doctor?"

"Hell, no. But that wasn't the question. Something about helping me get dressed, which is an offer that's hard to refuse."

"I'll get Hoolie."

"What's a Hoolie?"

"You'll like him," Sally said. "He's a cowboy, too."

"Do I have clothes somewhere?" Zach returned the lopsided smile. "'Cause if I don't have an outfit, Hoolie might not like me."

"We dried them." Ann transferred a short stack of neatly folded clothes from her sister's knees to the bed, about six inches from Zach's hand. Like she was afraid to get too close. "Actually, we washed and dried them. I hope you don't mind."

"No, that's great. Thanks." He could see he was going to have to ditch the subtle humor. She'd missed his little I-see-by-your-outfit joke. "I didn't think I was gonna make it. I remember that now. How far did I walk?"

"Three miles. We're three miles off the road, and it dipped down below zero last night."

"Hip still giving you trouble?" Sally asked. "I'm not in the business anymore, but I still watch and read all things rodeo. You know what I thought when Red Bull cleaned your clock that night?"

"That I was a dead man," Zach guessed.

"That I was an idiot. I sold that bull to the Chase Brothers when he was a yearling."

"He's been Bull of the Year twice." Zach grinned. "Congratulations. You've got yourself some good breeding stock."

"I sold most of that, too. In this business you either have to be a fortune-teller or a fortune inheritor. I inherited a dream, and all I can tell you is, you never can tell."

"Which is why you can't be counted out until you *are* a dead man." He laid his hand on the folded clothes. "I'll get myself dressed and see what I can do about getting out of your way this morning."

"No rush," Sally said as she wheeled back on one side for a turnaround. "I have business to attend to. When Hoolie comes in, send him back to the office, will you, Annie?"

Ann stepped aside for Sally's chair, manning the door as she spoke. "I have breakfast ready for you, and Hoolie wants to know whether to pull your pickup in."

"You got a can and a couple gallons of gas I could buy?" *At a dollar-fifty a gallon?* Unless they wanted to cash a check for him. He'd have to call the bank first, save himself from adding insult to injury.

"You can discuss that with Hoolie. He's already had a look at the pickup. I gave him your keys." She paused, doorknob in hand. "I hope you don't mind."

"No. That's…that's great. Thanks. Hey…" Zach gave a come-on nod, and Ann took a step in his direction. "Was Sally in an accident?" he asked quietly.

"No."

"I been on the circuit quite a few years now. I meet a lot of people. I know the name, but human faces kinda morph together. You know, like in some of those TV ads. I get a chance to look a bull in the eye, that's a face I don't forget, but people…" He lifted one shoulder, gave an apologetic smile. "Guess I've taken one too many kicks in the head."

"You couldn't offend my sister if you tried. She never met a cowboy she didn't like. If you've forgotten any of your career stats, I guarantee she can fill you in. She misses being part of it all." She smiled back. "But she's found something else."

"Yeah?" He took his shirt from the pile and shook out the folds.

"Yeah. Something just as wild. How do you like your eggs?"

"Cooked." He plunged his right arm into a sleeve. "I'm easy."

That made two of them. Ann had been scared he'd remember, scared he wouldn't. Now that it was settled, she could kick herself for caring, or she could take care of herself on the inside and maintain her cool on the outside.

Oh, yes, she certainly could. She'd learned a lot since her brief encounter with Zach Beaudry. She'd grown a lot. Actually, she'd shrunk quite a bit—at least sixty pounds' worth, although she wasn't one for stats—but she considered herself to be a bigger person than she was eight years ago, and exactly what she'd weighed when weight was a stat she had no use for anyway. Really. Back then she'd been dying her hair and using more makeup, following the advice of one transformation how-to after another. If she met her old self right now, she probably wouldn't recognize her, either.

Yeah, she would. Ann would know her by her fear, and she'd just had a flashback. That insecure little big girl was tucked away inside her now and always would be. She deserved to be protected. Zach Beaudry's poor memory left Ann's good one in control. Maybe she'd remind him, just to see how he reacted. Maybe she wouldn't. It would all play out soon enough, and it would be her call.

She was lining up the last dripping strips of fried bacon on paper towels when she heard the back door close. Hoolie Hoolihan announced himself with his signature two-note whistle from the mudroom, and she responded in kind. It was one of those routines that went way back. As far as Ann knew, her father had carved Hoolie from a Double D fence post and whistled him to life. That was the old hired man's story, anyway, and he was sticking to it.

"How's your patient?"

"He's out of the woods." Ann cracked an egg into the iron skillet, ignoring the gnarled, leathery hand that pulled a bacon soldier from her carefully arranged rank and file. "Soon to be headed for Texas."

"Not if he's countin' on the ride he left sittin' out there on the highway. Is he gonna let me tow her? Like I says, she was sittin' on Easy, but I gave her a little juice, and she still wouldn't turn over."

"You can ask him after you check in with Sally. She's back in the—"

"You can ask him now." He favored his left side as he ambled across the tile floor and stuck out his hand. "Zach Beaudry. You must be the man they keep referring me to. Hoolie?"

"Gas ain't gonna do 'er. You got Triple A?"

Zach chuckled and shook his head.

"The last guy we had broke down out here, he told me he had Triple A. One of them fancy foreign jobs. Good luck gettin' parts around here for one o' them babies. But he was gone next I looked, so I guess the Force was with him, huh? Satellite, beamer-upper, club card, something. 'Course, you wouldn't be freezin' your ass off walkin' in from the highway…"

"…if I hadn't left home without the card. Next time I'm takin' the Beamer *and* the satellite."

"You can always get a horse. You'll still freeze your ass off." Hoolie looked up expectantly, eyes twinkling.

"But it sure beats walkin'." Zach clapped a hand on the wiry old cowboy's shoulder. The men shared a laugh while Ann smiled to herself and tended to the eggs. "How much gas did you put in? I'm beginning to think she's got a hollow leg."

"I put in five gallons, but no go. I can pull 'er into the shop here and have a look later on. Long as she's American made, I can prob'ly get 'er goin'. Or you can use my tools if you're in a hurry."

"I'm on your schedule, Hoolie, thanks. Gotta say, I hope your schedule includes breakfast."

Ann took her cue to glance up. Zach smiled. *He was clueless, all right.*

"It did," Hoolie said. "Three hours ago. You walked in from the road with that gimpy leg?"

"Hell, no. I borrowed one of Annie's."

More instant-compadre humor.

"Ann." She slid two fried eggs on to a shiny white plate and presented it to Zach, who questioned her with a look. She gave a perfunctory smile. "It's just Ann. My sister gets a pass because it's better than what she used to call me."

"Gotcha. I got an older brother."

She added buttered toast to his plate. "Help yourself to the bacon."

He took two pieces.

"It's all yours," she said, and he claimed one more with quiet thanks as she turned to open a cupboard.

"I don't know how I walked in from the road, Hoolie," Zach said as he seated himself at the place she'd set at the breakfast counter. Some part of him gave an inhuman click, and he winced. "Feels like some of my replacement parts gave out. You got any extra sockets in your toolbox?"

"We can sure check." Hoolie turned to Ann and nodded toward the hallway. "How's she feelin' this morning?"

"Other than a little extra fatigue, given all the excitement, herself seems to be feeling herself." Ann handed Hoolie a cup of coffee. "But that doesn't mean she can take on the world, and don't you let her forget it, Hoolie. She listens to you."

"She wants to take in more horses."

"I know."

He shrugged, sipped, shrugged again, avoiding Ann's eyes. "She says the Bureau of Land Management is offering a pretty good deal on a one-year contract with extension options. We can handle a few more."

"Hoo-*lie,*" she warned as she grabbed another coffee mug from the open cabinet.

"I'm with you," he pled quickly. "We're full up."

"And when I'm not around, you're with her."

"Well, she can make a lot of sense when you're not around." Hoolie leaned closer to Zach's ear. "I try to please, but there's only one of me and two of them."

"You gotta love the one you're with," Zach said as he mopped a puddle of egg yolk off his plate with the corner of a wheat-toast triangle.

"I just do what I'm told," Hoolie muttered, head down, headed for the hallway. "Try to, anyway."

"Now you've embarrassed him." Ann set a mug of black coffee near Zach's plate.

"He knows I'm joshin' 'im." He closed his eyes and *mmm*'ed over his first taste of her coffee. She'd passed the ultimate test. He came up smiling. "How long has he been with you?"

"Hoolie came with the ranch. He worked for my father."

"So you inherited him?"

"Of course not." On second thought, her indignation dissipated. "I should have said Hoolie's with the Double

D. I don't know what we'd do without him. Maybe he inherited us."

"I guess I did embarrass him. *Love* can be a touchy word when it hits home. I thought he was just workin' for wages." He chewed on his bacon while she puzzled over what line he might have crossed between cowboys. "Maybe I can help him out today. I can't go anywhere until I get my pickup fixed. What kind of horses you run here?"

"Wild ones."

"The best kind." He sipped his coffee while she poured herself a cup. "Switching from bulls to horses?"

"We're taking in wild horses. We're kind of a sanctuary for unadoptable mustangs culled from wild herds on Federal land. They're protected by law, so they have to be put somewhere." She raised her green coffee mug in tribute. "Give us your old, your injured, your perennially rejected."

"Your *can't live with 'em, can't shoot 'em,*" he supplied.

She seated herself on the counter stool beside him. "If you're a rancher, your choices can seem almost that impossible. We used to be ranchers. Our father did, anyway. Now we're more like…" she thought for a moment, couldn't come up with anything better than "…a sanctuary. That's what we've become."

"You get paid to take in these useless horses?"

"The BLM helps with the upkeep, yes, but we're, um…"

"Doin' charity work?" He drew an air sign. "Bless you, sisters." And he grinned. "I really mean that. A buddy of mine works for the BLM out in Wyoming. Took me up in the hills one time, and we caught up with a band of mustangs. One of the prettiest sights I've ever seen. Usefulness is definitely overrated. Hell, look at me."

"You have wild horses in Montana, don't you?"

"Montana?" He looked at her, considering. She froze. He finally smiled. "Somebody's keepin' track of more than my rodeo stats."

"Well…" Her token smile bridged the gap between heartbeats. "That's what sports fans do."

"Were you a fan, too?"

"Not really." She lifted a shoulder, avoided his eyes. "I was in college when Sally got into the stock contractor business."

"You never went along for the ride?"

She could feel him studying her while she studied the tiny oil beads in her coffee. "You've seen one rodeo, you've seen 'em all, pretty much."

"Ouch."

"People get hurt. Animals get hurt." She looked up, suddenly brightening. "I do like to watch the barrel racing."

"Me, too. Pretty girls on great horses—can't beat a combination like that." He set his cup down and went after the last of his eggs. "What do you do, Ann? Besides take care of your sister and keep this place going?"

"I teach high school English and history. Sally's the one who really keeps this place going. I help her as much as I can."

"I like history. English, not so much. You gotta write. I don't mind reading, but I can't spell worth a damn." He took a bite of eggs, a bite of toast, chewed, watched her. "I figured you for a teacher. You got a familiar way about you. Patient." Without taking his eyes off her, he flicked the tip of his tongue over his lower lip and caught a crumb. "Forgiving."

"That's an odd thing to say. Most people don't—"

"Sally needs a ride," Hoolie announced at their backs, causing Ann a bit of a jolt. "She wants to take a turn around that northeast section while she's feeling up to it, and I got work to do."

"I'll drive her." Ann slid down from the stool, taking her coffee with her.

"I'll make a deal with you," Hoolie told Zach. "You drive the ladies, and I'll work on your pickup when you get back."

"I can take care of it, Hoolie," Ann insisted.

"Go on and show the man around. Show him what we've got goin' here. He'd enjoy the tour." Hoolie clapped a hand on his new buddy's shoulder. "Right, Zach?"

"Sure would."

Ann credited him with sounding interested. It was limited credit, considering his options were even more limited.

It felt good to be behind the wheel of a fully operational pickup. Good to be moving, especially when his body was dragging its tail. Zach hated it when his body acted pitiful. He was a firm believer in mind over matter, and believing had served him well for a good long time. Then along came the bad time, starting with a couple of cracked ribs. But taped ribs were all in a day's work. He was breathing normally by the time a plunging hoof had landed on his left foot. Bones too small to worry about hadn't been allowed to mend properly. Then came torn ligaments in his knee, broken fingers, fractured collarbone and horn-skewered hip. His buddies had comforted him cowboy style, telling him how he'd looked when Red Bull tossed him in the air "like a short-order cook flipping a pancake." He hadn't seen it that way himself, but that was what he was told. Cowboy humor. When it hurts too much to laugh, your friends'll do it for you.

The damn bull had used an ice pick on him instead of a spatula. But it would be a cold day in hell before he'd let a bull have the final say on Zach Beaudry. He'd come close again, but it turned out he hadn't hit bottom. He hadn't landed in hell or anywhere near death's door.

And a cold day in South Dakota was hardly unusual, unless you weren't used to a high, wide, handsome sky the color of a bird's egg and air so pure you could smell God's fresh-hung laundry. The rolling hills and jagged buttes were swathed in a dull patchwork of brown-and-tan stubble. Frost feathers clung to the drooping heads of tall prairie grass, and silver-gray sage was the closest kin to anything evergreen poking out of the sod. There was no road to follow—only cow paths, tire tracks and Sally's orders.

"Head for high ground," she sang out from the far

side of the pickup cab. Zach noticed a slight tremor in the gloved hand directing the way.

Straddling the gearbox hump, Ann must have noticed, too. Without a word she laid a solicitous hand on her sister's knee as Zach arced the steering wheel and tipped the two women in his direction. Sally brushed the hand away. It was a subtle but telling exchange, and Zach had no trouble reading the "tell." *It's my hand, my play.* He reached across Ann's knee, downshifted and put the pickup on an uphill course, following two parallel ribbons worn in the sod. He let his jacketed forearm linger a moment past necessary. *His* tell, for whatever it might be worth. *Tenderness noted, Angel Ann.*

They topped a rise and stopped, silently surveying roughly twenty horses strung out along the draw below. Their coats were thick and dull, their manes shaggy and tangled, their bodies clad in prairie camouflage—dun and grullo and palomino, spots the colors of rocks and ridges, tails like grass.

"Good," Sally said after a moment. "We're downwind. But they'll sense our presence soon enough. See that bay stallion?" She pointed to a stout, thick-necked standout. "He's a Spanish Sulphur Mustang. We just sold some of his colts. Got some good money for them even though horse prices are down. He's getting a reputation for himself, which helps pay the bills."

"How many acres you got here?" Zach asked.

"Five thousand, but we're bidding on a lease for fifteen hundred more."

Ann stiffened. "We are?"

"I told you, didn't I? I can't believe it's available. Along the river on the north side." It was Sally's turn to pat a knee. "It's *water,* Annie."

"We'd have to get more domestic livestock, and we can't handle that. We don't have enough help, Sally."

"More rodeo stock?" Zach asked.

"More cattle," Ann said. "We're a balancing act these days, running steers and just enough of a cow-calf operation to call ourselves a ranch. Horses don't qualify as farm animals in this state. Without the domestic stock we'd pay much higher property taxes."

"So we'll get a few more," Sally said. "We're officially nonprofit now."

Ann sighed. "That's for sure."

"Which means we're satisfying the federal side. I've got the balancing act under control, Annie. And I have a few new ideas in the incubator." Sally leaned for a look at her driver. "Aren't they beautiful?"

"No doubt." Zach scanned the jagged horizon. "Pretty piece of land they've got here. They fit right in."

"They belong here as much as we do. *More* than we do, but they have to depend on us these days."

"Can't tell by lookin' at 'em."

"Which is the way it should be," Sally said. "Have you ever seen the holding pens the culls end up in when there's no place else for them to go?"

Zach nodded. "I've seen pictures. They're well fed."

"They're sad," Ann said quietly.

"Horses are born to run." Sally gave a sweeping

gesture across the dashboard. "That's who they are, and they know it. The wild ones do, anyway."

"So you're just giving them a place to live free. They don't have to do anything but be themselves."

"Pretty much. We sell as many of the colts as we can. I wish we could afford to put more training into them. I know our sales would improve." Sally leaned forward again, peering past her sister. "How much horse sense do you have, Zach?"

"He's a cowboy, Sally. Of *course* he knows horses."

"Do you, Zach?"

"Been around 'em most of my life, one way or another. Can't say I ever owned one, but I never owned a bull, either." He smiled. "I'll ride anything with four legs."

"But you want your ride to buck," Sally said cheerfully.

"That's the only way I get paid." Zach nodded toward the scene below. "I'm like them, I guess. I know who I am." He glanced at Ann. "Is that what they mean by horse sense? Having as much sense as a horse?"

"It's about being practical," Ann said, slipping her sister a pointed look.

"In that case, I've probably got some catchin' up to do."

"You're not the only one," Ann said quietly.

"Mount up, Zach. My little sister will soon have us up to speed in pursuit of practicality."

Again he nodded toward the herd. "If that's what practicality looks like, I'm mounted and ready for the gate." One by one the horses began raising their heads, ears perked and seeking signals. Zach chuckled. "Who calls the play?"

"The wolf," Ann said. "They know he'll show up sooner or later, and they're ready either way. And that's horse sense."

"How do you like my little sister, Zach? Makes you think, doesn't she?"

"Whether you want to or not." He caught Ann's eye, gave her a smile and a wink. "Maybe that's why she's in better shape than both of us put together, Sally. Ready to fight off the wolf when he comes to your door."

"Or hold him off while we take flight." Sally chuckled. "In our dreams."

"Oh, for Pete's sake," Ann complained. "Obviously somebody's going to have to run this bunch in today so we can cut those two skinny old mares out and that gelding. They won't like it, but they're not getting enough to eat."

"Where's that kid of yours who's supposed to help out?"

"Wherever he is, he's using up his lifeline."

"We get help from Annie's students," Sally explained. "Some are more dependable than others."

Ann nodded. "The sanctuary is a community service. Kids get in trouble, they can sometimes do their time here. Most of them do very well, and some of them even come back as volunteers. We had five of them off and on last summer. It's a good program."

"Pain in the patoot," Sally muttered.

"It's my patoot," Ann said. "I know how to take care of it."

Zach laughed. "I like your little sister just fine, Sally. Just fine."

He liked their layout, too. If he'd done what he'd planned to do when he'd had the money—and he'd been in the money for a while there, had a few stellar seasons—he'd have his own place. He'd had his eye on a little ranch near San Antonio, but it had gone to developers while he was still playing in his winnings.

His brother, Sam, had won some big money not too long ago, or so he'd heard, and he wondered how Sam was spending it. But he kept his wondering to himself. Sam was one of the "more dependable than others" kind. He showed up when he was supposed to, did his job without risking his neck, banked his paycheck and paid his bills on time. Hard to imagine him buying a lottery ticket, but if anybody could pick the right numbers, it would be Sam.

When he'd asked Sam to buy his share of their grandfather's land, Sam had tried to talk him out of it. Said he'd loan Zach what he could to get him started on the professional rodeo circuit, the PRCA. Zach hadn't cared about land back then. He'd been a high school bull-riding champion, and he was going down the road wearing brand-new boots, driving a brand-new pickup. Sturdy, skilled, strong-willed, he had what he needed. *Ain't nothin' gonna hold me down or cramp my considerable style, bro.*

Except his own body.

He'd been sitting too long, and the notion of hitting the road anytime soon wasn't sitting too well with his diced-and-spliced hip. *You're gonna pay for all that walkin' last night, son. Your body and your truck were all you had to look after, but you beat up the one and deserted the other.*

He watched the Drexler house grow in appeal as much as in size as the pickup drew closer. He thought about the warm bed behind the first-floor corner window. He wouldn't mind laying his aching body in it for another night. Being held down was no longer much of an issue. Getting up was the challenge.

He dropped the women off near the back door and headed for the outbuildings, where his beloved Zelda stood powerless, her bumper chained to a small tractor hitch like a big blue fish on a hook. Hoolie pulled his head out from under Zelda's hood and wiped his hands on a greasy rag, which he stuck in the back pocket of his greasy coveralls. A disjointed memory of his father flashed through Zach's mind as he parked the Double D pickup nose to nose with his own. Greasy coveralls had looked damn cool through a little boy's eyes. If it was broke, Dad could fix it.

"You got some engine trouble here, Zach," Hoolie said. Like after last night, trouble was news. "I could use some help gettin' her into the shop, but I can tell you right now, she ain't goin' nowhere unless she gets a good overhaul. Rings, seals, the whole she-bang. Not that you weren't runnin' on fumes, but who needs a gas gauge when you've got that second tank?"

"That's what I say."

"How long since you've had 'em both full?"

"Since gas was under a dollar a gallon. How long ago was that?"

"I ain't that old, son." The old man smiled. "Tell you what. You help me out around here, I'll fix your pickup for you. Don't give me that look. It's a simple American-made straight shift. I can order parts off the Internet, slicker'n cowpies." He did a two-finger dance on an imaginary keyboard, tweedled a dial-up signal, made a zip-zip gesture and smacked the back of one stiff hand into the palm of the other. "In one tube and out the other, sure as you're born. Hell of a deal, that Internet."

"Haven't used it much myself."

"You gotta get with the twenty-first century, boy. For some things. Others, hell, you can't beat a handshake and an old-fashioned trade, even up. I help you, you help me."

Zach nodded. "What do you need?"

"A good hand. All-around cowboy. These girls got a good thing goin' here, but they're runnin' me ragged."

"Good for what?" Not for profit, according to the "girls."

"Good for what ails us in the twenty-first century. Tube-headedness. All input and no output. Too many one-way streets. Too much live and not enough let-live."

"Gotcha."

"So, what do you say?"

Zach glanced under Zelda's hood. *Poor girl. Mouth wide open and she can't make a sound.* In their prime he'd made sure she had nothing but the best. A guy had no excuse for neglecting his ride. "You're a pretty decent mechanic?"

"Worked for my dad until he closed up shop. Then I came to work for Don Drexler. Every piece of equipment, every vehicle on the place runs like a top."

Zach smiled. "I say I'm getting the best end of the deal."

Chapter Three

Zach eyed the amber-colored pill bottle sitting on the corner of the dresser. He hadn't taken any last night. He'd had himself a long, hot bath instead. Then he'd taken Ann up on her offer of an ice pack and a heating pad, and he'd been able to sleep without painkillers. He often woke up feeling like he'd aged considerably overnight and needed a crane to lift him out of bed. But when the pain lay deeper than stiffness, he cursed himself for putting the pills out of reach.

When *damn you, Beaudry* didn't cut it, biting his lower lip and blowing a long, hot *f* made pushing out the rest of the word his reward for hoisting his legs over the side of the bed and erecting his top half. One bad word begat another. Pain radiated from his hip to all parts north and south. It was his focus on the pill bottle that bolstered him through the threat of a blackout.

"Zach?"

It was the giver of hot and cold, come to get him up and at 'em. She'd heard. She was thinking up another remedy. *Tap, tap, tap. Here's an idea.*

"Yeah!"

"Are you…okay?"

"Yeah."

"Do you need—"

"No!"

"Okay." Silence. "I can send Hoolie up."

"No." *Don't be rude, Beaudry.* "Thanks."

"I could fill the bathtub."

He closed his eyes and bit down hard on his lip, listening. She was still there.

"Yeah." He drew an unsteady breath. He hated himself when it got like this. A few pills and he could sink back down and sleep the day away. "I'll…I'll do it."

"It'll only take a minute, and then I'll leave you to—"

"Yeah!" She means well. She's sweet. Remember sweet? "Yeah, that'd be great."

A few minutes later, she knocked again. He was staring at the pill bottle.

"It's ready."

"Thanks."

"I'm leaving for school in about—"

"Okay. Good. Later."

"Are you sure you can—"

"Yes!" Mind over matter. It was the only way. "Once I get movin', I'll be fine. Can you just…go away?"

"I'm going." Pause. "There's breakfast."

"Great. Thanks. 'Preciate it."

He counted her retreating steps. No way could he get those jeans on until his joints loosened up. He hadn't worn pajamas since he was about eight, and he wasn't planning to until he was at least eighty. That left the flowery purple quilt.

Warm water was a godsend. When it turned cold he felt as good about being able to climb out, flex his knee, bend at the hip and pull the plug from the drain as he had sticking his first bull. There was hope. It was a new day.

He savored the smell of smoked bacon chasing the aroma of hot coffee down the hall, and he followed it through the dim foyer, past the stairs—where he claimed his hat from the newel post—past the Christmas tree that stood as a dark silhouette against a window filling slowly from the bottom with pink light. Nothing stirred except a calico cat, who slit-eyed him as she gave a full-bodied stretch across much of the sofa.

He found Ann sitting alone at a little kitchen table. No plate in front of her, none of the bacon that had lured him by the nose. She looked up from the stacks of papers she was having for breakfast with her coffee. The soft gold curls that had graced her shoulders a few minutes ago were mostly caught up on the back of her head with a few left to frame her pretty face. He was glad she hadn't left yet. She had a warm, welcoming kind of smile. Reminded him of someone. Probably not a particular someone, but the sort of someone he sometimes got all sentimental over. Had to be careful not to hang around that kind of smile too long.

"You look a lot better than you sounded earlier." She slid lined paper full of kid-scratch from shrinking to growing pile, smiling all the while at him. "I take it you're not a morning person." She nodded toward a coffeemaker on the counter near the sink. "Help yourself."

"Some mornings are better than others." He plucked a cup from a metal tree with one hand and pulled the carafe from the coffeemaker with the other. "It was a long, cold walk brought me to your door, and cowboys don't like walkin'. These boots ain't made for it."

"According to Hoolie, your legs aren't shaped for it."

"Whoa, now." Coffee in hand, he did a bow-legged about-face, kicking up the charm with half a smile. "A lotta girls admire this shape. Ain't easy to come by."

She gave the smile back in equal measure. "The *girls,* or the shape?"

"What do you think?" The look in those blue eyes said she'd spare him the answer. Such courtesy was too much to expect from the noisy bum that was his left knee, but he needed a reminder to quit playing cute. Still, he wasn't above voicing an *ouch* to further his case with her. "I feel like…" *like we've met somewhere before, which is the worst line in the book* "…like you're not most girls. *Women.* Sorry." He shook his head. "I'm feeling a little awkward, like

I'm missing something. God knows, after what happened the other night..." He chuckled. "I probably don't wanna know, huh? Couldn't've been much dignity in it."

"Some pieces should just be allowed to go missing."

The way she said that gave him a chill. He'd made an ass of himself for sure. He took his hat off and sat down across from her anyway. She was probably right, but she was definitely making him curious, which was an impulse he'd schooled himself to resist, especially when it involved a woman.

Low resistance was probably a side effect of hypothermia.

He slid his hat under the table and set it on the seat of an empty chair. "When does Hoolie usually show up?"

"He made breakfast. He wondered when you might be showing up." She slipped the smaller stack of papers inside a red teacher's book. "I told him there were some strange sounds coming from the guest room. Agony or ecstasy—I wasn't sure which."

"You had the cure." He watched her pile the book on top of the other papers, took it as a hint. "I'll just take my coffee and head on out to—"

"Let's have some breakfast," she said, all warm and bright again as she shoved her work aside. "I have a bad habit of skipping it, but I have time. Hoolie's the earliest of early birds. After about five o'clock he loves to accuse the rest of us of sleeping late."

"I made a deal with him. If he's out there workin', I need to be out there, too."

"Not without breakfast," said a voice from beyond. Sally rolled her wheelchair onto the kitchen linoleum. "If a rancher doesn't feed her help, word gets around."

"Not so much in the off-season," Ann said as she rose from her chair. "How are you doing this morning?"

"The spirit's more than willing, but the body could use a boost. You know what I'd love? Besides coffee."

"A bacon-and-cheese omelet?" Ann flew to the refrigerator like she was magnetized. "We've got mushrooms and tomatoes. I could—"

"A cool bath. Did you turn the heat up last night?"

"I don't—" Ann slid Zach a questioning look "—think so."

He shook his head. He figured he was back up to his regular ninety-eight point nine.

"I'll run the water for you," Ann offered, backing off the omelet with a note of disappointment.

"You'll do breakfast. I just wanted to make sure everyone was finished with the bathroom."

"I only used one towel," Zach reported. "The wet one."

"Thank heaven for hydrotherapy, huh?"

"Amen to that, sister." He took a cue from the look in Ann's eyes. "Followed by a little protein."

"Save me some bacon. Did I hear you say you made a deal with Hoolie?"

"If it's okay with you, I'm gonna help out around here while Hoolie works on my pickup. He offered, and he says it shouldn't take too long for him to fix it once we get the parts. So I'll be his right-hand man until Zelda's up and runnin'. Couple days, maybe?"

"Fine by me," Sally said, laughing as she reversed her wheels. "Zelda?"

Zach shrugged. "She generally treats me better when I call her by her right name."

"Gotta love a guy who names his pickup."

"Can't take credit. It came on her license plate. ZEL-412. Zelda B. Zelda Blue." He grinned. "But I'll take all the love I can get."

"You got it, cowboy."

Sally left them to a quiet kitchen. Zach wanted her back. She was like him—not quite whole and not too worried about it as long as no one acted like they should be.

"You've been together a long time," Ann said finally. "You and your…Zelda."

"For sure." Good topic. "Bought her brand-new. Top of the line. She's been good to me, I'll say that."

"Until now?"

"My fault." He waved away any blame that might jinx Zelda. "Been runnin' her ragged, not keeping up with the maintenance she deserves."

"Sally calls her wheelchair Ferdie. Ferdinand the bull."

She said it softly, with a wistful smile. Sure sign she was about to tell him something he didn't want to know.

"What about you? You got a name for your ride?"

"Gas hog."

Keep her smiling. "Is it a sow or a boar?"

"It's an *it*." Here it comes, ready or not. "My sister has MS."

Clearly a good citizen would know what the letters

stood for right off, and Zach was reduced to raking his brain for words that fit. He knew the name of every bone and major muscle in his body, having damaged most of them, but he wasn't planning on getting into diseases for at least another thirty years.

"Multiple sclerosis," she said, gently filling him in. "It affects the nervous system, and every case is different, so we really don't know what to expect. During remission, sometimes you can hardly tell there's anything wrong. But the last remission wasn't quite as long as we're used to." She sipped her coffee. "This relapse has been harder than the last. More stubborn. Sally's a strong woman, always has been. She doesn't ask for help unless she has to. She thinks she should be looking after me."

"Seems like she's not tied to the wheelchair. Like yesterday, she was…"

Ann nodded. "Yesterday was good for her. Thank you for that."

"Hey, the pleasure was mine. I mean, I enjoyed it. I sure didn't do much. But I would." Where was he going with this? *Would what?* "Just tell me."

"I have to go to work." She stared at him as though she expected him to make the first move. "As soon as I leave, Sally's going to want to get out and get her hands dirty. She wore herself out yesterday, and she'll be pushing it again today. Because you're here."

"Me?"

"New blood. A transfusion from the life she loves. She misses watching her bulls buck boys like you into next week. I don't doubt that whatever Hoolie has in store for you today, Sally'll be itching to get in on it. And she got too hot last night, which isn't good for her. It weakens her muscles."

"All I wanna do is help out, Annie. Hoolie's bound and determined to fix my truck, and while he's doing that, I'll just be one of the hired men. Nobody's gonna be itchin' to wrestle me for the manure fork."

"We don't have hired men. *Hired* implies a regular paycheck."

"Like I said, Hoolie's gonna—"

"I know." She raised her palm in surrender, sighed, said almost inaudibly, "I know. Hoolie does his best. And my sister—"

"Forgot her coffee." Sally was back.

Zach smiled. With the help of a cane she was off the wheels. Faster than spring runoff, Ann was pouring the coffee.

"I don't see any food in front of this man, Annie."

"Ain't much of a cook, but I can do eggs," Zach said. "I can do eggs all around."

"I have to get—"

"No way, Annie. I know your schedule, and you've got time." With a nod of thanks, she took the coffee Ann handed her. "And by the way—" Sally sipped "—if I feel like doing some chores, I'll do chores. If I feel like getting on a horse, I'll saddle up. I don't need any—"

"Permission, I know. I'm sure you and Zach will enjoy trading stories over your eggs. If either of you decides to get on a bull, please hold off until I get home."

Ann gathered up her papers. "I love a good butt-busting."

Zach looked at Sally. "Man, she's cold."

"As cold as they come," Sally said. "Fortunately, I'm still in charge here. Right, Annie? I'm the senior partner."

"Good sense trumps age, senior sister. I'm only giving one assignment here." Ann pointed at Zach. "Keep her out of trouble."

"Yes, ma'am." He winked at Sally. "Shouldn't be too hard, huh? One troublemaker to another."

Ann wasn't surprised when Kevin Thunder Shield didn't show up for her first-period class at Winter Count Day School, but his mother Margie's visit at the end of the day was completely unexpected. Ann and Margie did not see eye to eye when it came to fourteen-year-old Kevin, who had done well enough working with the horses as a summer volunteer that she'd tried to keep him involved by hiring him for a few hours a week year-round. Unfortunately, Margie made too frequent a practice of playing Kevin's advocate, and Ann was ready to bow out.

She rose from her desk chair and braced herself for some tortuous case in answer to a simple question. "How's Kevin?"

A tall Lakota woman of commanding presence, Margie folded her arms beneath ample breasts and drilled Ann with dark, challenging eyes. "I just found out today that he wasn't out to your place over the weekend."

"He was a no-show Saturday morning, so I wrote him off for yesterday, too. I've asked him to call if something comes—"

"Cops picked him up last night." Margie made the announcement without discernable emotion. "I went to court with him today. Him and that bad bunch he's been runnin' with got into big trouble."

"I'm sorry, Margie."

"You shoulda' called me when he didn't show up to work."

"I assumed you—"

"All that time I thought he'd gone out to your place after school Friday. How do I know he's not there if you don't call me?"

"I wasn't expecting him Friday," Ann repeated patiently.

"I know that now, but he told me you were. He was staying over, he said."

"I'm sorry." Ann bit her tongue against expanding on her apology. She was sorry about Kevin, but it was hard to regret not calling his mother when she'd suggested more than once that Ann's terms were unfair, that she should pay him more. "I wasn't sure where we stood. I should have checked on him, but frankly, I didn't have time."

"He lied to both of us, then. Maybe I should just…" Margie unfolded her arms and tucked a strand of black hair behind her ear. "I talked a deal with the judge. If you're willing."

"The job's still open, if that's what—"

"It's more than that. We were thinking, the judge and me…we think he could work for you, like, every day. Stay at your place and work off his sentence in community service. Weekends, too. He'd go home with you after school on Friday, and you bring him back to school Monday morning. So he'd be, like, way out in the country and totally in your custody on weekends. He can stay there as much as you're willing to keep him. You just keep paying what you been paying, but you keep out room and board and pay the rest to the court. He owes eight hundred dollars." Margie lifted a shoulder. "He don't eat much."

Ann tucked some sympathy into a smile. "He does after a few hours of stacking bales."

"I can send some—"

"What does Kevin say about this?"

Margie turned toward the open door and called her son's name.

Kevin made no apologies. He neither shuffled his feet nor hung his head, and he met Ann's knowing gaze with an easy return. He knew her, too. She hadn't counted on him, but neither had she given up. At fourteen he was allowed to be a work in progress.

"Miss Drexler wants to know what you have to say for yourself."

Kevin hitched up his baggy jeans. "I missed work, missed class this morning because I got into something Friday night. Started out with a few beers, ended up bustin' into a car nobody was using. Been sittin' there in front of Alfred Iron Necklace's house for a year. Just wanted to see if I could get it to run. All I did was bust a…" He glanced at his mother, who had been staring out the window, having heard it all before. "Ain't done nothin' fun since school started. No parties, nothin'." His mother continued to ignore him. "They're my friends," he insisted. Still nothing from Margie.

"I'm not sure where I fit into all this, Kevin," Ann said.

"Didn't my mom already—"

"No, *you* tell me what you're proposing. This isn't between your mom and me."

He took a moment to put it together. "Okay, the judge thinks we should do some kind of contract, like you've got for your classes. Everything I earn goes to restitution, and I gotta do nothing but go to school and work for you. Judge figures it could take me to the end of the school year. I can handle that. I like working at your place, and I don't wanna get court-ordered to some juvie program or Indian boarding school."

"What *do* you want, Kevin?"

"I wanna stick close to home. Go to my same school, do good in school, *finish* school and make something of myself."

Ann nodded. The boy knew what his teacher wanted to hear. "That shouldn't be hard for you. You're smart, and you're a good worker when you put your mind to it."

"And those *friends* you're talkin' about are too old for you," Margie said. "Which is why the judge is giving you this chance, because she knows they were using you. And plus, everybody knows some of those guys are into drugs."

"It was only Beetle and Bad Dog, and they don't do drugs. The car was my idea," the boy claimed. "I didn't try to weasel out. They shouldn't've even got—"

"You don't worry about them!" Margie ordered. "They're all out of chances, those two." She slid Ann a pleading glance.

"It was your idea to get involved with us last summer," Ann reminded him. "Is this contract your idea?"

"Yeah. I still wanna help you with the horses."

"What you want is to stay close to home, go to school here, work at the Double D," Ann reviewed. "Oh, and make something of yourself."

"Yeah."

"And stay out of jail," his mother added.

"That, too." Kevin grimaced. "Barnyard manure smells better than jailhouse puke."

"These are your choices?" Ann glanced at Margie. "I hate to think we're just the lesser of two stenches."

"I can do the work without complaining, Miss Drexler. I don't mind getting my hands dirty. I just get tired of Hoolie raggin' on me all the time."

"That sounds like a complaint already." Ann gave a perfunctory smile as she reached for her canvas book bag.

"Okay, okay. Whatever he says."

"I'll talk with Hoolie about it tonight."

Margie reached inside her coat and produced a manila envelope. "I need you to sign a paper for me, Miss Drexler. Otherwise…"

"Right now?"

"I have forty-eight hours to get the plan signed, sealed and delivered back to the judge."

"Then I have forty-eight hours to think about it, talk it over with my people and get back to your people." She loaded papers, plan book and text into her bag before checking in with an eye-to-eye. "Right?"

"Can I…" Kevin glanced at his mother, but this time he was on his own. He returned to his last-best chance. "Maybe go with you to talk to Hoolie? I just wanna tell him myself, like, I know I prob'ly said some things that sounded a little—" he made a seesaw gesture "—disrespectful, maybe. I didn't mean it like that. Maybe he could use a hand right now. Did he get those horses moved?"

"He may have. He had some extra help today."

"A volunteer?"

"A rodeo cowboy we found half-frozen on our porch."

"You hired him?" Kevin sounded hurt.

"Hoolie's fixing his pickup." She could have said *yes*. She could've nodded and kept her mouth shut. But, no, she had to let a perfectly good teachable moment slip away, right down the bleeding-heart tube. She laid her hand on the boy's lean shoulder. "He won't be around long, Kevin. We still need help we can count on."

"You can totally count on me, Miss Drexler. Seriously, let me talk to Hoolie."

"*I'll* talk to Hoolie. You get to my class on time tomorrow morning. With Friday's assignment and the one you missed today, both *done*." She jotted down some page numbers, handed him the paper, and then turned to Margie. "I'll let you know tomorrow."

"You wouldn't have to pay him anything."

"The question is…" She glanced at Kevin. It didn't matter what her question was. On the heels of a troubled weekend he was set to say the right words. "I'll have our answer for you tomorrow."

Zach was impressed with Hoolie's computer savvy. By day the old man walked and talked all cowboy. But tucked into the corner of the efficiency bunkhouse—a renovated line shack from the ranch's early days—with its Roy Rogers decor was a computer center any geek would have been proud to call home. He could shop, communicate, get the news, make new friends while keeping up with the old and put twentieth-century throwbacks like Zach to shame. He could even tell whether Sally was online to receive a message, which she wasn't, and whether she'd picked up his last message, which she hadn't. As pleased as he was with being "connected up," he enjoyed assigning message delivery to his new helper even more.

Zach knocked softly on Sally's door.

"Enter at your own risk, Hoolie. I'm loaded for bear."

"No bears and no Hoolie." Zach opened the door wide enough to get his head through. "Don't shoot. I'm just the messenger."

Sally shoved what looked to be a stack of bills to the front of the desk that was home to another computer. "I'm surprised you're still here."

"No wheels, remember?"

"If you're entered up somewhere down the road, you'll find wheels."

She wasn't smiling, but he laughed anyway. "You know your cowboys."

"Never had one of my own," she told him. "Never wanted one, to tell you the truth. Kinda like a mustang."

"You got plenty of those."

"They're not mine. They stay here because they've got no place else to go."

Rather than claim he had places to go, he gave a tight smile. Once the hint was thrown down, he wasn't one for pushing his luck around a woman in a touchy mood.

"What's the message?"

"Hoolie wants to order a part for that eight-end tractor and a new pump for the stock tank before it snows. He's ordering some parts for me, says we can save on shipping."

Sally stared at the pile of papers. "How much does he need?"

"He says four-fifty should cover your end."

"Don't I wish." She stared silently for another moment, but when she looked up at him, the cloud over her dissipated. She slapped the arm of her wheelchair and chortled. "My end is way too big for this damn sling I've gotten it in." And then, amazingly, she sang, "I've got my ass in a sling, hangin' from a rain-boww. Got the sling cutting off the circulation in my fing-gerr." She offered up a warm smile. "But what can you do besides hang tough?"

"That's all I know." He smiled back, relieved. He didn't much like the thought of Sally hanging.

"I've been keeping the books for almost a year." Her deep sigh made it sound like a lot longer. "Annie did it for a long time, and she was good at it. I took over so I could be useful from a chair. The ol' sling. The ol'…" She stared at the bills again and shook her head. "I don't fit the damn chair. I don't fit the job. Nothing adds up, nothing balances, and nothing works."

Zach shoved his hands into the back pockets of his jeans. What could he say? "My parts aren't in with the four-fifty."

"I know." She gave a mirthless chuckle. "Tell Hoolie to get what he needs."

He started to turn, and then his brain kicked in. He knew how she felt, and she knew… "You get used to your body operating a certain way, and then it quits on you and you don't know who you are anymore." He shrugged. "Your parts don't add up."

"You look whole."

"So do you. But I'm not doing what I want to do right now, and neither are you."

"Speak for yourself, cowboy. I'm doing it. Just not quite the way I thought I would." She splayed her fingers on the pile of papers. "But I do need more time. More money." Her eyes met his, and she wagged a finger. "More help."

"Like I told Hoolie, I'm able and more than willing, long as I'm here." Sounded big of him. Like he could've left already, but here he was. He smiled. "He's got me lined up to fix the fence, and if I don't quit burnin' daylight, he's liable to withhold supper."

"Go." She smiled back and waved him on. "Earn your keep."

"You need anything? You want me to—"

"I have a phone." She eyed him, one wounded warrior to another. "You know what I *don't* need, Zach. Probably better than anyone else around here."

"Right." He paused again. "I admire what you're doing for the horses."

She nodded. "I love to watch them run free."

Chapter Four

"What we don't need around here is another project."

Hoolie was digging in his heels at the supper table, and Ann was beginning to wonder whether her unspoken status as his sentimental favorite was going to get her anywhere with him this time. Kevin Thunder Shield had exhausted the limited benefit of Hoolie's doubt months ago. Hoolie didn't much like Kevin's kind. Teenage boys. He'd offered to camp on the porch and drive them off with his shotgun when the Drexler girls were teenagers.

"When he's good, he's very, very good." Unbidden, Ann passed Hoolie the meat platter. "Especially with the horses. He has a way with them."

"Sometimes," Hoolie allowed as he speared a

breaded chicken breast. "But if I can't depend on a guy, he's got no way with me."

"He's only fourteen. He's still learning."

"Well, you're the teacher, little sister. Not me."

"I know. I shouldn't expect…" She shouldn't do this right now, either. Suppertime was traditionally downtime at the Double D. "But Kevin's at the point right now where all he needs is a nudge, either way. Very good, or very bad. This could be the crossroads for him, Hoolie. This chance, this time and place, we might make the difference. It can't hurt to give him one more chance."

"It can't?" Hoolie glanced at Zach. "She's never been a fourteen-year-old boy."

"They can do some damage, all right." Zach nodded as he tore into his bread.

"They can do twice as much damage if they're still boys at twenty-eight," Ann said. "As any woman can tell you."

"Bring me one of them twenty-eight-year-olds, I'll put him to work. As any man ever worked with me can tell you." Hoolie gestured with his table knife. "Like Zach here. He's all broke in. He can barely see boyhood in his rearview mirror. Right, Zach?"

"Some might say it's closer than it appears," Zach said quietly.

"Not with all them lumps you've taken."

"Now, wait a minute, Hoolie. You been peekin' through a keyhole? I'm thirty-two."

"I'm just sayin' some boys don't grow up without a few hard knocks. That boy, Kevin, he's a hardhead. I got no time for hardheads. Hell, I'm *seventy*-two. I got no time for keyholes or mirrors or fancy talk. I see what I see, and I know what I know."

Seated directly across the square table from him, Ann challenged Hoolie with a look. "Meaning I have to turn the Thunder Shields down?"

He laid his knife on the edge of his plate. "You don't have to do nothin' on my account, little sister. You're the boss."

"Put Zach in charge of him," Sally suggested from the left. "Annie's in charge of Hoolie, Hoolie's in charge of Zach, Zach gets to ride herd on Kevin, and you've got yourself a set of Russian nesting dolls."

"How do you figure Russian?" Zach wondered idly. "You got two Indians in the mix." Catching Hoolie's look of surprise, he added, "My dad was Metis."

"Is that one o' them new casino tribes?" Hoolie asked.

"It's one o' them old mixed-blood people who couldn't decide whether to swim or fly."

"So you walk," Ann said, tempted to add a comment about how he'd said his boots were made. She remembered something he'd said that long-ago and nearly forgotten night about being part Indian, but she hadn't known what to make of it, hadn't asked him to elaborate. Everything he'd said that night had filled her with wonder. For her part, she'd said nothing without weighing, measuring and trying to squeeze the artlessness out of it first.

"Wander," Zach corrected with a subtle wink. "The old ones did, anyway, and some of us still do. No fins, no wings. And when you got no wheels, it's boots on the ground."

"This sounds like an interesting history lesson," Sally said.

"Don't know much about his-sto-ry," Zach crooned, ending on a lopsided grin. "But I do know I'm part French and part Chippewa on my dad's side. His people were trappers and traders and buffalo hunters on both sides of the Canadian border. Didn't want to be lumped in with whites or Indians. Said they were a new people who deserved the benefits of both, and they tried to back it up, tried to make a stand back in the frontier days like everybody else. In Canada they pretty much got neither. In the U.S. they got some on-the-way-to-nowhere land in North Dakota and Montana, which is not the best location for a casino. But, hell, you take what you can get." He raised his brow. "We ain't rich, but we're damn good-lookin'."

"You can say that again." Sally grinned.

"Nah, once is plenty." Zach chuckled. "We're re-lated to the Cajuns down South. They got Bayou, and we got Big Sky."

"Fish *and* fowl," Ann said. "You'll be welcome at almost any table."

"Never thought of it like that." He gave her an ap-preciative smile. "So the hunger I see in some peo-ple's eyes…"

"Like you said, it has everything to do with how good you look."

Sally laughed merrily as she passed the platter of

chicken. "Don't let any of this get *by you,* Hoolie. It's absolutely delicious."

Ann delighted in her sister's rare pun.

Hoolie picked up on the chicken. "Can we go back to the part where Zach takes charge of that kid?"

"Would it help me get my pickup fixed quick and cheap?"

"You bet."

Zach leaned back for better access to his pocket and his keys, which he slid across the table into Hoolie's territory. "All in. How long do you think it'll take?"

"Oh, I'd say about as long as that kid stays around."

"I said *quick.*"

"And I said you could bet on it."

A full belly and empty hands drove Zach into the cold night for a smoke and solitude. Not that he needed either, but they fell in line whenever he felt out of alignment. Which, lately, he did more often than not. He lit up, and then he buttoned up. Damn, it was cold. *South Dakota.* South of what? The North Pole? The wind was so cold and sharp it was about to bore a hole through his chest.

More likely it was whistling through one that was already there. He took a long, slow drag on his cigarette, deep enough to put a burn in his chest, a tingle in his fingers and an itch in his cold clay feet.

Way to go, Beaudry. You offer to help some good people out, and then you start looking for excuses to bail.

He blew a cloud at the stars as the door opened and

closed behind him. He felt a rush that had nothing to do with nicotine. A competing itch. He stared at the stars as he stood pat, anticipating that first jump, the one that would set the direction. Out of a dozen possibilities, he had it down to two—either *show me what you've got* or *this is where you get off.* He was ready, either way. The match was always the most exciting when the chances were even.

"Are you all right?"

All right? Why wouldn't he be? Leave it to a woman to come up with possibility number thirteen.

"Exposure lowers a person's resistance." She closed in on him from behind, moving slowly. "We had you at a disadvantage."

"You think so, huh?" He turned. "Nobody puts Zachary in the corner."

Either she didn't get it or didn't care to. She gave his cigarette the evil eye. He returned a cool gaze over a long, slow draw on his smoke. "I smoke 'em if I got 'em." He studied the ash end protruding between curled fingers. "I'm almost out."

"My grandmother died of lung cancer."

"Sorry to hear that."

"She didn't smoke. She was stuck in a house full of people who did."

He nodded, straightened, started toward the steps.

She grabbed the sleeve of his jacket. "No, it's okay."

"No, it's not okay. Your house, your rules."

"I don't make rules, really." Her hand came away, and she stepped back. "What I meant to say was that—" she gave a nervous titter "—we don't hold people hostage here."

"I'm too close, and you're uncomfortable." And he was calling her like he saw her. *Who had who at a disadvantage?* "I'll help out any way I can as long as I'm here. Is that okay?"

"Kevin's a good kid, but he'll test you."

"Sure he will. And I'll pass, easy. Unlike you and Hoolie, I got no skin in the game." He lifted one shoulder. "So to speak."

"What are we speaking? Martian?"

"Man talk."

"Exactly."

She pulled her long dark coat together in front—he imagined buttoning it for her—and hugged herself to keep it together. He imagined doing that for her, too. Give him time. He'd get there, long as he kept his head in the game. Skin would come later if she wanted to put up half.

He took a drag on his cigarette and blew it over his shoulder.

She mocked him, blowing vapor.

Sweet.

"Since when did you take up smoking?"

"You make it sound serious." He eyed her over one last drag. *Since when* struck him as curious, but he shrugged it off. Curiosity was a distraction. "It's not. Only thing I can't do without is my pickup." He flicked the butt over the porch rail. The red coal arced, plunged, shattered like a kid's sparkler.

"Well, I'm sure your pickup will be in good running order soon after the parts arrive. Hoolie can fix anything."

"One of the parts is on back order."

"Hoolie doesn't think Kevin will last long. I think he will if we give him a fresh start, which is where you might be able to help. Without putting any skin on the line, of course."

"In the game," he corrected her. "Sounds like the boy's back's against the wall. That's what it takes sometimes." He shoved his hands in his jacket pockets. "Rodeo's a young man's game. I meet a lot of kids on the circuit. Skin's nothing to them, but *try*, now, that's something else. If they're gonna wash out, you can tell pretty quick. It's at least ninety-five percent attitude. You run outta try, you say bye-bye." He chuckled. "I'm betting you'll know within a week whether it's you or Hoolie's got the boy pegged."

"Betting what?"

"A week."

"Putting your time where your mouth is," she reflected.

"Yeah." He grinned. "In return, you put food in my mouth and a pillow under my head."

"What about Texas?"

"It'll still be there. Let me see what I can do here in a week."

"Hoolie was going to keep you around as long as he could anyway. He likes you." She glanced toward the outbuildings. "He needs help."

"How about you?" He waited until she turned to him

again. "You don't have to ask. I'm here, and I'm offering. But I don't have to be here if you don't—"

"It's between you and Hoolie. And Sally. I'm not Sally. I can't do nearly the job, the *many* jobs she's always handled herself, and Hoolie..." She sat down on the porch railing. "Ah, Hoolie. I'm afraid I take him for granted. He's been working here for as long as I can remember. The Double D is as much his as it is ours." She looked up at him, lifted one shoulder. "As much as it is *mine*. Sally's the heart and soul, and Hoolie's the life's blood. I'm just a Drexler. I'm part of that second *D*."

"Sally talks up your end of the deal the same way. Says you're the brains of the outfit."

"She told you that?"

"Pretty much." Damn. She'd opened herself up, but he'd gained no ground. And he wasn't itching. He offered his calloused palms. "With two ranch hands, your major body parts are covered."

"For a week."

"Hey," he said amiably. "One day at a time."

"Works for all my parts except the one." She glanced past him. "The brain has to consider the bottom line."

Smiling, he lifted his hand to touch her shoulder as though he were smoothing a wrinkle, giving her leave to step away. When she didn't, he touched her hair and then her temple with two oddly tentative fingers. "Give it a rest."

The following morning Zach beat Hoolie out of the gate. His first chore was chopping the encroaching ice in the corral tank. He wondered if he could rig up a homemade solar panel that would give the tank heater a fighting chance against the north wind. It was something he'd read about and tucked away in his mental to-be-tried file. He had a lot of try left in him, and one of these days he planned to start using it in new ways. Before he started losing his files.

Between the barn and the kitchen he crossed paths and exchanged a little happy talk with Ann, who was on her way to school. *Damn.* Missed his chance for a nice warm-up. He had to keep a closer watch on the time. Maybe he'd even get himself a watch.

He enjoyed his second cup of coffee with Zelda, who was cold and quiet, but her cab was his cab. He could peruse the pages of the *Bear Root County Chronicle* without having to explain his attachment to a pile of back issues of an eight-page local newspaper from the upper reaches of Montana. It didn't make much sense for a constant traveler to take a subscription of any kind, but Zach had a post office box down in Texas and a friend willing to manage the spare key. She tossed the junk, read the occasional real piece of mail to him when he called, and filed issues of the *Chronicle* in brown paper bags marked with dates, which he hauled away periodically.

He dipped into his hometown news infrequently. He had to be in the right mood—neither under the weather nor over the moon. He needed to be able to search the pages of the papers for familiar names without feeling the urge to call in like some lovelorn trucker listening to a late-night oldies radio show. So here he was, shivering in South Dakota, turning pages and muttering a phrase now and then, wondering what was on sale at Allgood's Emporium, his mother's country store, and what her book club was reading this week. If it wasn't some hard-luck Oprah pick, maybe he'd get himself a copy. He was finding more time to read these days. Books had a constant quality about them, a solid feel. A real connection.

He turned the page and scanned for names of the county's most reluctant guests, hosted by his own big brother, Sheriff Sam Beaudry. Were any of Zach's early bronc-bustin' buddies enjoying Sam's no-nonsense company? Zach hadn't gotten real serious about rodeo until after Sam left home, and unless his brother had discovered cable TV somewhere along the line, he'd only seen Zach ride the handful of times he'd showed up in person. Sam had walked on water, and then he'd walked off into the sunset, leaving Zach to figure out how to get from boy to man on his own.

He'd been invited to Sam's September wedding—offered the role of Best Man—but he'd phoned in his toast. Ma was mad as hell, and she had every right to be. Zach had left a hole in the damn program. He'd screwed up his hip again and could hardly walk, but he kept that information to himself. He wasn't one to waste a call on excuses.

Sam hadn't said much. Thanked him for calling. Introduced him over the phone to the eight-year-old niece he'd never met. Told Zach not to believe everything he heard about Sam winning the lottery, that the money mainly belonged to his daughter and some good chunks of it had gone to charity. Zach hadn't heard. It had been a while since he'd picked up his mail.

The lottery. Unbelievable. Real people didn't win the lottery. Zach tried to imagine Sam leaving a trail of money behind him wherever he went. When that image didn't gel, he tried thinking about Sam with a wife and kid. He could see a woman and a child—glossy-haired, bright-eyed magazine material—but he was still having trouble fitting Sam into the picture. The man Zach had worshipped after their father died—Sam had had no trouble growing up fast—was still a hero, still a hard act to follow, and still way out there, a silhouette on the distant horizon.

"We oughta take a drive out to Bear Root, Zel. It's almost Christmas. Good time to visit family, huh?" He rubbed the curve of the steering wheel with a gloved hand. "Right."

His half-audible conversation was interrupted by a knock on the window.

"Breakfast?" Hoolie shouted.

Zach raised his coffee mug.

"You're gonna need more than that."

Zach set the paper aside and emerged from the truck.

"We'll be moving stock, and it'll take us past your usual dinnertime."

"I don't have a usual dinnertime, Hoolie, but thanks for the warning. Horses?"

"That's the only way we get around our pastures. You can leave your ATV at the Double D gate."

Zach gave Zelda's blue hood an affectionate pat. "This is the only four-wheeler I own. I meant, are we moving horses?"

"It'll take more than the two of us to move them mustangs. They move whenever they feel like it. No, we're bringing the heifers in closer. I don't like the turn the weather's taken."

"I'm with you there." Zach fell into step with Hoolie, who was headed for the barn. So much for breakfast.

"Too damn early for winter watering. The older I get…" Hoolie flipped the latch on the door to the tack room and held it open for Zach. "Damn, I hate ice."

"I'm with you there, too."

"Had one go down on a frozen stock dam and break her leg last year. Couldn't get her up. Had to shoot her." Hoolie pulled an old roping saddle off one of the heavy pegs attached to the wall in three vertical rows. "Coulda' been me."

"Now, that's where we part company." Zach chose a saddle with sloping swells and a low cantle. "Don't shoot. If I go down, just leave me to my misery."

"Hell, you're a cowboy. That's three letters smarter than a cow."

"*B-o-y* doesn't add up to much in the smarts department."

"Smart enough to know a good thing when you land on her doorstep." Hoolie raised his free hand as they headed for the corral. "I'm just sayin', these things happen for a reason."

"Ann? I really don't think she likes me much."

"I coulda been thinkin' Sally." Hoolie clucked to a black gelding, extended his free hand and waited to be sniffed. "Don't worry. I wasn't."

"Nothing to worry about." Zach set his saddle down, front end on the ground, and eyed the two remaining saddle horses, a black mare and a bay. "I'm keepin' my boots under my own bed."

"Annie's the quiet one. What is it they say about still water?"

"Runs deep and dangerous." Avoided by the black, Zach walked right up to the bay, who took the bit in her mouth like a piece of candy. "But, yeah, I've thought about her some. *Ann*. She won't let me call her Annie."

"You run wild and dangerous. She's afraid to like you too much." Hoolie gave his cinch a good pull, clucked to the black to take a few steps and release the breath he was using to puff up his girth and add some inches to the cinch. "I worked for their dad. Watched the girls grow up. Helped them bury both their parents. Annie's always been real tender-hearted." He jerked the slack in the cinch and secured the end—slip, slap. "From the time she was about three years old they had to send her to stay with her aunt when we shipped calves. Couldn't bring her back until the cows stopped cryin' around for their babies. You know what that's like."

Zach grunted as he swung his leg over the saddle, answering more to the hitch in his hip than Hoolie's assumption. He called himself a cowboy, but in truth he had little interest in bovines without balls. Back in his early days on the circuit he'd hired out when he had to—mostly on custom combining or haying crews—but wages weren't his style.

"Sally was right in there, helping us round up the herd, working the chutes, taggin' along to the sale—that girl loved every minute. But Annie took it like cows were the same as people. Too much Disneyland, you ask me."

Zach rode through the gate Hoolie was ground-tending, smiling as he pictured Ann skipping down a cartoon road wearing a red cape, red bow in her hair, whole herd of baby animals trailing after her. If he stayed on, maybe she'd pay him in gumdrops.

"We could use your help around here. More than just babysittin'." They were loping across a flat, horses' legs swishing through dry grass, Hoolie jawin' away, hardly missing a beat. "You got plans for Christmas?"

"Plans?"

"Some people think about where they're gonna be. They call it *plans*."

"I generally think about it, but somehow the time just slides by."

"Your gate," Hoolie announced as they pulled up to the first fence line.

Zach was just getting comfortable. He rolled down to the tune of squeaking leather.

"You got family?"

"My mother's in Montana. My brother, too. Haven't been back in a while," he confessed as Hoolie rode past him. "My plans are tied to the circuit." He dragged the wire gate away from the post. "Somewhere down the road there's a bull savin' the best eight seconds of his ornery life just for me. For all I know those eight seconds could be part of December, what? Twenty-fourth? Twenty-fifth?"

"How long since you made the whistle?"

"Date, time, who keeps track? It's what I do. Bulls fear me." Zach muscled gate post snug against fence post, hooked the wire loop from one to the other, and squinted up into the sun. "Women don't."

"Ain't sayin' she's afraid *of* you. She's afraid *to like* you. She's particular."

Zach harrumphed as he mounted up.

"Hell, she's like these mares we got around here. Real fussy about who they trust."

Zach tapped his heel against his mare's belly. "Can't work for somebody who don't trust me."

"Can't trust a guy till you get to know him some. With a woman, it takes more than eight seconds."

"Nobody tops a woman off that quick." Zach laughed as he adjusted his hat against the sun. "Not at our age, anyway."

"Speak for yourself, boy." Grinning, Hoolie stood in his stirrups. "Nowadays, they've got a pill for everything."

"Yeah? How's that workin' for you?"

"That'd be tellin'. But like they say, you gotta ask your doctor if you're healthy enough. You keep forkin' them bulls, boy, you get to be my age, won't be a question of *how* but *if* they're hangin'."

"Nowadays, they've got body armor for everything, but thanks for the concern."

"Just tryin' different buttons."

Zach eased the mare into a rocking lope. "I said I'd stay a week."

Hoolie's gelding tested the bit, eager for a race with the mare, but the old cowboy checked his mount and kept his case on track. "We could use your help through the winter."

"This isn't what I do, and it doesn't pay what I used to…" *Damn. Think positive, Beaudry.* "What I'm used to."

"*They* could use your help."

Helping out was one thing. Hiring on was something else. He didn't want it, and *they* couldn't afford it. Why couldn't he just be a guest doing his host a favor?

Because if he didn't get a move on and put a screeching halt to his losing streak, he'd be down to two options—wages or favors.

He eyed Hoolie and set his mind on some straight talk. "If it wasn't for this kid, I don't think she'd want me here even a week. Kinda feel like it's personal."

Hoolie chuckled. "Tell you what. Try callin' her Annie again. If she don't get her back up, you can take it personal."

"That's not enough. You're talkin' Christmas, and that's nearly a month away. Requires an invitation. Beyond what we've agreed to, I want to be asked." He stabbed a gloved finger in Hoolie's direction. "And without you puttin' any bugs in anybody's ear."

"Sally's sure to—"

"We ain't talkin' about Sally."

"Annie's as proud as you are, boy."

"Good. That's good." Zach stared straight ahead. They were a match, all right. Attitude-wise, they were at least ninety percent. "Maybe I don't have plans, but I've got plenty of options that don't include any part of a South Dakota winter. But put me to work for as long as I'm here, Hoolie. I'm no freeloader."

"Last winter was mostly open. Ain't seen a hard winter around here since…" Hoolie adjusted his hat against the sun. "Can't rightly remember."

"I hear they've got a pill for that, too."

Chapter Five

If there'd been any chance he was looking at more than a week of what the Drexlers were calling *fall weather*, Zach might have taken Ann up on her invitation to go to Rapid City for some shopping. He would have gone with her to do almost anything else, but he wasn't much for shopping, could hardly get in and out of a store fast enough. His jacket wasn't arctic gear, but he could pile on a few layers, and he had a good supply of wool socks. He'd be okay for a week as long as he didn't have to wear his cowhide gloves when he was shoveling manure. He just wished the rawhide pair he'd gotten from Hoolie weren't such a tight fit.

He decided to stop wishing and turn them over to smaller hands, along with the manure fork that went with them. Not that Zach wasn't holding up his end of the job—hauling was no more appealing than forking—but he assured young Kevin that the gloves had been molded to fit the fork handle.

"I'm doing this to stay outta jail," the boy grumbled as he emptied the fork of its smelly load. "What's your excuse?"

"I don't make excuses." Zach flexed his hands in a pair of canvas gloves he'd found on a shelf in the toolshed. They'd do in a pinch, which was what he was in for. "We have a job to do, my man."

"You should be doing this part. You're the one getting paid."

"Am I?"

"Drexler says Hoolie hired you."

"Drexler?" In the interest of picking his battles, Zach would have let this one go if the kid were referring to any other teacher.

"Sorry. No disrespect. *Miss* Drexler. You know, the hot one." Kevin looked up from his forking with a twinkle in his eye. "So *that's* your excuse."

"There's that word again."

"Tell you right now, you won't get anywhere with her. She ain't interested." Into the wheelbarrow he tapped off another forkful, smiling now. He had the goods. "She says you won't be around long."

"Here's the deal. If you wanna stay out of jail, you've got a week to prove yourself. To me." Zach raised a gloved point-maker. "Rule number one, no disrespect. None. Seriously." He raised an eyebrow. "Rule number two, no excuses. None. Seriously. And Ann didn't say Hoolie hired me, which brings us to rule number three. No lies." A few seconds' worth of sink-in time. "Deal, or no deal?"

"Like I told Drex—Miss Drexler—I'll take this place over jail. Or getting sent away. I'm not afraid to work." Kevin shrugged and gave an apologetic smile. "I was just yankin' your chain about Miss Drexler. She's the kind you don't wanna mess with too much."

Zach nodded. He knew the pecking order was a work in progress, but all he had to do was keep at it. "Tougher than she looks?"

"She'll totally stand her ground, but she's pretty fair. Some teachers really get off on writing people up for any little thing, but she's not like that. She's one of the good ones. You don't wanna make trouble for her."

"Agreed. The good ones are hard to find. If anything, you want to make things a little easier for them."

"She says you're a cowboy." Kevin cocked his head. "You look a little Indian to me."

Zach blew a stream of steam. "Bigger than you, and don't you forget it."

"I'm a lot Indian. Where you from?"

"Montana. My dad was from Rocky Boy. I guess I'm about as much Indian as cowboy. You ride bulls for a livin', they call you a cowboy."

"Your dad still lives up there in Rocky Boy?"

"He died a long time ago."

"Mine left, too, but I don't think he's dead." A second thought brightened the boy's eyes. "Matter of fact, we think he might be in Montana. Up around Rocky Boy. Heard he's got a new woman. We could be related by now, you and me."

"I haven't had much to do with…" Zach caught the change in the boy's expression in time to switch gears. "I don't go around shakin' family trees."

"Then you're not much Indian."

Fair enough, Zach thought. Indians knew their place among their relatives.

"How'd you end up frozen on the Drexlers' porch?" the boy wanted to know. He read the challenge in Zach's eyes and added, "That's all she said."

"Pickup trouble."

"Oh, yeah. Hoolie's fixin' it for you. Good luck with that."

"I taught you a thing or two about your basic gas-powered engines, didn't I, boy?" Hoolie's voice drew their attention toward the door standing open to the corral.

There he stood, all ears, eyes on Kevin. "Heard you got caught tryin' to get one runnin' without a key."

"It was a junker. Been sittin' there since—"

"Guess a thing or two adds up to a little learning," Hoolie opined as he rolled the track door closed. He turned, grinning. "Which sure can be a dangerous thing."

"That's part of the learning curve for some of us," Zach said. He wondered whether Hoolie'd ever looked in the mirror when he was grinning all smug. It didn't look good on him. "You learn a thing or two, you gotta try that dangerous thing before you're ready for thing three. Whatever doesn't kill you makes you stronger."

"Where is that on the curve?"

"The dangerous thing? At the intersection of smart-enough-to-know-better and too-stupid-to-live." Zach winked at Kevin. "And don't try to tell us you haven't been there, Hoolie. You're about as strong as any man I've met."

"I've been lucky once or twice." Hoolie gave a gotta-admit-it bob of the brow. "But it's mostly skill and sense. You can't count on luck."

"He's right about that, Kevin. Good skills and sense can improve your luck, wherever you are on the curve. So keep workin'."

"I think I've got this skill down," Kevin said as he slid the fork under another target.

"Cleaning the barn is a chore. It don't take much skill, but there's some sense involved. Enough to know it has to be done. It's about being in it for the long haul. Endurance. Right, Hoolie?" Zach clapped his gloved hand on Hoolie's shoulder. "You talk about a long haul, this man is amazing. Looks pretty good for a hundred and five, don't he?" He squeezed, and Hoolie gave a quick laugh, rubber-duck style. "He's been damn lucky, and more than just a time or two."

"Matter of fact, I'm feelin' pretty lucky right now. I get to let you two make the long haul out to the manure pile." The old man grinned. "Tomorrow I'll show you how to spread it."

"Shee—"

"With the tractor," Hoolie added.

Kevin's curse cooled. "Can I drive?"

"And I've got an idea I'd like to show you guys, see

what you think." Zach tucked a glove under his arm to free up his hand for a dive into his file folder—the back pocket of his jeans. "The new pump works good, but if it gets much colder, that little heater won't be enough to keep the water open in the stock tank out here." He nodded toward the door to the corral and shook open a folded piece of paper.

"It's too small," Hoolie said. "We've got a bigger one, but it give out last winter, and I haven't been able to fix it. A new one costs an arm and a leg." He peeked over Zach's arm. "Can't spare those right now."

"I drew this up. No arms, no legs. All I need is some scrap wood, some kind of insulation." He glanced up, nodded for Kevin to come take a look. "You heard of solar heat?"

"Sure." Kevin looked surprised, like a rookie called in cold off the bench. "They put up some kind of panels to trap heat from the sun. They heat whole buildings."

"If they can do it, we can do it. Paint this part black to hold the heat better." Zach looked at Hoolie. "You got some glass around here that's not doin' nothin'?"

"Don't sweat the small stuff or throw away the stuff that's still good," Hoolie recited. "You get ready to make something, you got scraps for materials and sweat for glue." He assured the boy with a glance. "That's what we call cowboy ingenuity."

"What's to keep the animals from breaking the glass?"

"Good point." Zach tapped Kevin's shoulder with the back of his hand. "See, that's why I'm bringing you two in on the design phase. You'll help me figure something out." He cocked a finger at Hoolie. "Supply." And Kevin. "Demand."

"Demand what?" Kevin asked.

"Answers. Solutions." Zach smiled. "You keep those questions coming, young fella."

Ann's plan was working. *Seemed to be* working. Okay, so far, so good. Four days' worth of good. According to the Lakota—among whom she was both student and teacher—four was a good number. Kevin had been eager to get back to the ranch on Friday— *Friday!*—because he was going to get to drive the tractor. She'd worried aloud about his age, but a male voice in each ear telling her to "quit worrying" had convinced her to step back and watch the men steer the boy through a rite of passage on big, bumpy tires. For all their enthusiasm, she could have sworn they were all fourteen, but she couldn't help smiling at the cheers for a successful clutch release after a series of engine kills.

During supper, there was talk of Kevin getting a "farm kid's permit." After supper, he volunteered for more chores.

Ann used coffee as an excuse to get into Sally's room, where her sister was hard at work on the computer—a good sign that she wasn't exhausted, a bad sign for business. Sally was either swamped by expenses or finagling a way to accumulate a few more. No surprise, it was the latter case.

"We can make this work, Annie. The way I figure

it…" She brought up a spreadsheet and scrolled through it slightly slower than she talked, considerably faster than the speed of Ann's mental calculator. "I know we can lowball our bid on the new lease. There's more land available than they can find takers for, and this parcel won't attract anybody but us. I'm almost sure of that." Eyes on the screen, Sally made an insistent gesture toward a chair.

"There's water on it. Everybody needs—"

"But it's isolated. Hard to get to. Perfect for us. We could take on another two hundred horses."

"Two hundred!" Ann plopped into the chair.

"And once we get this parcel, we'll be next in line for this piece over here. Look." Sally's mouse nosed Google Earth on to the computer screen, flew over familiar territory and dove for Sally's target like a bat out of heaven while she narrated. "Because who's gonna want that when it's tucked behind these buttes, and we've got all this? And it's really not much good for anything but—"

"Coyotes and wild horses, I know."

"Don't forget the rattlesnakes and prairie dogs. Maybe we could bring in a few buffalo."

Ann groaned. "You're figuring in the cattle, right? We'd have to add cattle."

"We can do it, Annie. All we need is a few more friends. I'd say *hands,* but I can't find much more room on here for…" The spreadsheet emerged from the screen's bottom line.

"Payroll?"

"Yeah." Sally scrolled up and down too quickly for any serious searching to be done. They both knew what was there. But Sally turned a beseeching eye on Ann anyway. "Any way we could tap into the household budget?"

"I'll look it over." Ann's standard answer.

She had agreed to let Sally take over the books for the ranch, claiming that separate bookkeepers for business and household would make for smooth fiscal sailing. Neither of them believed it—the Double D would always be as strapped for cash as it was land-locked—but the tacit agreement to pretend to believe protected Sally's pride, thereby serving them both. Ann didn't have to say, and Sally didn't have to see that the medical bills were eating up the household account. Not that Sally didn't know without looking or that Ann didn't show without saying. *Feelings will out* was one of Mother's mottoes according to Sally, self-proclaimed keeper of the memories. And unspoken emotions ran high on the medical front. Untold fear and undue guilt. If there were some way Ann could get her sister on her health insurance program, all would be well.

All except Sally, who would never be well.

"This sanctuary is going to be a model for natural set-asides," Sally insisted. "I know we can do it, Annie. We were meant to make it happen. It's just simple as that."

And just that impossible for Ann to deny.

So she didn't try.

With Sally sleeping and the men reportedly playing cards in the bunkhouse, Ann found time for her kind of simplicity. She built a fire in the fireplace, dropped a couple of cinnamon sticks in a small pot of apple cider, and set about stirring up the holiday spirit. Her mother had left a cache of decorations that represented generations of family milestones, and it was Ann's job to unpack, restore, display and carefully put them away every year. Sally knew the pieces' histories, but Ann claimed the privilege of putting them out in old and new arrangements, making up legends in her own mind as she went along. She had names for all the sheep, glittering dance partners assigned to all the nutcrackers, porcelain figures grouped into choirs and glass ornaments sorted by color. She took her time putting them out. They were like returning friends, appearing in small bunches from the day after Thanksgiving through Christmas Eve.

For Ann, the hanging of fresh greens marked the official transition from fall to winter. She made sure all the hooks were in place, organized her materials, brought the stepladder into the living room, and stood back sipping cider while she considered her plan.

"Man, it smells good in here."

Ann turned to find Zach watching her from the front hallway. "I brought the pine boughs and cedar back from Rapid City," she explained as he approached. Her need to explain was inexplicable, as was the urge to elaborate. But they were alone, and he was walking the walk, and she couldn't stop talking the talk. "We used to have a real tree, but they're a lot of work, and you can't keep them up as long. I like to keep the tree up through January for the lights. I get…"

"Winter blues?" He gave a knowing smile. "Me, too. This is about as far north I go in the winter."

"Even for Christmas? But you're this close." She measured a scant inch between thumb and forefinger. "Bear Root's about a day's drive."

"You sayin' my week's up?"

"I'm saying you'll probably want to pay your mother a visit."

"Got nothin' to drive. Far as I know, we're still missin' a part." He slowed at a comfortable distance from where she stood and then took another step. He smelled like pine smoke. "I s'pose Hoolie's been reading my mail." Her dubious frown made him smile. "That pile of Bear Root County newspapers I've got in my pickup," he explained. She didn't know what he was talking about. "I never said anything to you about Bear Root, did I? Or my mother?"

"Is she doing well?"

"Sure, she's fine."

"How do you know?"

"I call." He lifted one shoulder. "Sometimes. Christmas, for sure. But when I leave here, I'm headin' south."

"Cider?" She lifted her mug for show, but he put his hand over hers and guided her drink to his mouth. "It's hot," she whispered.

"Mm." He pressed his lips together. "I'll pass."

"Would you like something else?" she offered, and he shook his head. "You're welcome to stay through the holidays. A week was your bet, not mine."

"Maybe I was hopin' you'd raise me." She gave him a quizzical look. "Try it," he challenged, his eyes mesmerizing hers. "Aren't you curious?"

"What would happen?"

"That's not the way the game is played. You gotta say, I'll see your week…" he lifted his hand slowly toward her hair, moved a barely visible strand with a barely moving finger "…and raise you all the way into the next."

"I can't afford you…" she couldn't move, as his cool finger touched her cheek, trailed tingles to her chin "…that…long."

His kiss was impossibly tender. A touch of warm breath, a taste of spice.

An all-knowing smile. "Yeah, you can."

She stared at him. "How can you be so…"

"So?" He raised his head slowly, his eyes soft and suggestive. "That was nothin' but nice, Annie. If you're looking for an apology, you won't find it here."

"I'm not," she clipped as she stepped back, her eyes never wavering. She would not blink first. "I was, but I'm not anymore. My curiosity is satisfied."

"I don't buy that."

"How many days are left on the table?"

"Who knows? *You're welcome to stay* sounds like an open-ended bet. Your house, your rules." He grinned, glancing over the top of her head. "Thought it would be fun if I could get you to raise me."

"Maybe I should call—" she handed him a coil of garland "—your mama. Let her know what a gambler she raised. Betting his life away a week at a time."

"Wouldn't surprise her," he said offhandedly, inspecting the greens as though he were trying to figure out whether to eat the thing or wear it.

"It's like a rope." She showed him the end and made an unwinding gesture. "Maybe not the gambling itself, but you're betting your time on a troubled boy instead of a troublesome bull, that part might surprise her."

"She knows me better than that." He glanced up from his admittedly prickly assignment. "Sometimes I get the feelin' you do, too."

"I'm learning."

He feigned spinning a lasso before giving her a sweet, lost-boy smile. "What are we doing with this?"

"There's a hook on the corner of the window there. Do you see it?" She claimed the other end of the garland and the three-foot stepladder. "Can you reach it without a boost?"

"Does a bear crap in the woods?"

"Yes, I see how tall you are." She climbed up two steps. "There's a hook at the midpoint of the window, so we're going center…" She anchored her side end with two feet left hanging from a corner hook and then hopped off the stool to get the long view. "Okay, let me see. Yours is too long."

"How can you tell?" He reached for the hook.

"I peeked. Can you give me about six more inches?"

"No problem." He stretched—arms up, out, back up. "With inches to spare."

"Six is all I want right now. We want to come out pretty much even."

"Sounds good. You need more, just gimme some kind of si-i-iignnnOhgaawd."

Arms up, body rigid, he looked like a kid playing "Statues" who'd been jumping when "freeze" was called.

"What?"

"Come," he gasped.

"What!"

"Come. Get. This."

"Coming."

"Hurry."

She tried to take the garland from his grip. "Drop it, Zach. What hap—"

"Five seconds to the damn whistle," he ground out. "Get the damn ladder."

She grabbed the ladder, hung the greenery and gave him a shoulder to lean on before the signal sounded, which turned out to be tuneless air sucked between his teeth.

"What happened?"

"Threw my knee out." His first step was a hop. "Punishment for a smart-ass."

She tucked into his weak side. "Maybe you shouldn't try to do machismo and masochism at the same time."

"Don't make me laugh. If I go down, you're comin' with me."

"Can you make it to your room?"

He nodded toward the seating area in front of the fireplace. "I can make it to that sofa."

He knew he could have made it on his own, but he also knew how foolish he looked hopping around on one leg. And he liked the feel of her arm around his waist, especially on the heels of a soft, sweet kiss.

"How can I help?" she asked, touching him inside and out. Not the kind of touching he'd been laying the groundwork for, but he welcomed all overtures. Something about Ann was like coming home.

"It's like when you get a headache, you know? I'm not…" *Crippled* came briefly to mind, a word he'd basically ditched when he'd realized how close he'd come. "I'll be okay by tomorrow."

"Ice? Heat? What can we try?"

The notion that they might solve his problem together made him smile. "Ice, if you have it."

She helped him take off his boot—the hole in the toe of his brown wool sock was a little embarrassing—propped his leg up on the coffee table, brought him an ice pack and a cup of cider "just to try," stoked the fire and climbed up the ladder to hang a small wreath at the center of the pine garland they'd hung together. He enjoyed simply watching her move, up and down, sure and sweet. She made pleasure in ways he didn't wish for, ways that didn't fit with his program. It had been a long time since the combined fragrances of pine in all its glory—fresh-cut wood, green needles, sap and smoke—had pleased his nose. He'd nearly forgotten how comforting hearth-and-home scents could be.

She joined him on the sofa, refilled his cup from a green-and-white stoneware pot and poured a cup of cider for herself. The cups matched, and the green pattern reminded him of the pine boughs strung around the room. Funny he should notice.

"You're off to a great start with Kevin," she said.

"How can you tell?"

"Nobody's said otherwise. I'd hear about it if things weren't going well. Kevin seems happy. Hoolie's not *un*happy. You're still here." She looked up at him and smiled. "I'm thinking, three's company."

"Kevin feels safe here. Hoolie still feels like top dog. And I'm easy."

"Would you stay longer if we could pay you more?"

"Longer than the week I bet, which, depending on when it started, is up or just about." He stretched his arm along the back of the sofa, behind her head. "It ain't the money. Well, it is, but not yours. It's the prize money I need to be winning. You don't ride, you don't eat. And I'm not ready to stop eating."

"There are other…"

He shook his head. "I'm not ready to retire."

"Your body might disagree with your mind on that point."

"It's all about attitude. I've got a goal in mind."

"Just one?"

"One at a time. I know some people can handle more, but me, I get to thinkin' about too many things, I generally pay a price." He peered into his cup. "Which is kinda why I'm here. I'm off my game."

"Maybe it's time for a new game."

"Gotta win this one first."

"You've won it many times over. According to Sally, you've been very successful."

"Made the finals a few times, but I've never…" He looked into the fire. "Success in my business is winning the championship."

"Now it's a business. You just called it a game."

"It's both. It's also a profession. I'm a *professional* rodeo cowboy."

"And your goal is to win the championship?"

"Or die tryin'."

"These are your choices?" She adjusted the ice pack on his knee. "Must be a guy thing."

"I'm good at it. I've been riding my whole adult life, and I've made a lot of money doin' it." He glanced at her. "I know it's not like the work you do, but it's a sport that entertains a lot of people, and it takes real skill."

"I know. I've seen a lot of—"

"I'm good at it, Ann. I'd like to…" he turned back to the fire "…show you." Damn. What was he doing walking out on a limb with a bum knee?

"I've seen you ride, Zach. I know you're good at it."

Really? "How long ago?"

"Eight years, maybe nine."

"That long ago, you remember one eight-second ride?" *If that?* "Did I last eight seconds?"

She nodded. "Oh, yes. You certainly did."

"Good." He'd been hell on wheels back then. Winning his share of the money and then some, placing with almost every ride, showing his considerable stuff without holding back out of fear or tamping down pain. "Just one time?"

"I went with Sally. I was just finishing up at the university, looking at graduate school. Back then I wasn't really involved with the ranch."

"Bookworm, huh? I probably met Sally—met so many stock contractors, and I know the Drexler name—but you…" He wanted to see her eyes, but they were avoiding his. "I'd remember you."

"No, you wouldn't. I looked a lot different then."

"Well, hell. I did, too, but—"

"No, you didn't. I recognized you right away." She smiled into her cup, and he imagined her reflection in cider. "On the porch. Even with pale skin and blue lips."

"Embarrassing as hell." And sinking fast. "I *did* meet you somewhere along the line, didn't I?"

"You did, yes. At a party."

"I was big on parties in those days. These days, not so much." *Of all the rodeos and all the parties and all the women…* "Tell me I wasn't ripped."

"You were celebrating," she said quietly, distantly.

"So I made the whistle and won the go-round. Good, good." So far. "Where was it?"

"Omaha."

"Great venue. Love Omaha." Drop it there, he told himself. Back away. What's that saying about the better part of valor?

But no. "You're holdin' out on me here, and I feel like a real jackass," he confessed against the judgment he'd all but abandoned. *Might as well finish the job.* "Were you with somebody? Did I say something? Do something really stupid?"

"*I* did something really stupid."

"Hey, no problem. I missed it. I must've been…" He set his cup aside, turned to her to let them start over from scratch. "I don't remember much about how I got here, but I'll never forget seeing you through the window."

She stood abruptly, started across the room, spun around and gave him a strange look. "Can I get you a heating pad?"

"No, I'm…"

She turned and fairly lunged for a wall of cabinetry, swooped down near the floor, withdrew a small book from the shelf and marched back to the sofa, resolved. She sat down, opened the book and handed him a photograph. A test. A dare. "Do you remember her?"

He glanced. Well-rounded young woman in the T-and-A department, striped hair cut short and way too sassy for her…soft…sweet… He raised his eyes slowly. "This is you?"

The fire crackled and hissed.

Her eyes didn't waver. Her lips didn't move. They didn't have to. They were forever Ann.

He lowered his lyin' eyes and looked, really looked. "Your hair sure was different."

She laughed. It was an easy, honest laugh, as intimate as a kiss.

He stared at the picture, and the image came alive for him. She stood alone in the shadows, played with her hair—tugging at one side, trying to straighten it or make it grow—and he remembered wondering whether she was wearing a wig.

"That's right," she said quietly. "In the midst of all that celebration you were feeling quite charitable that night."

"You look younger now than…" He waved the picture between them. "But you were *in college.*"

"I was old enough, yes."

"I'm sorry, Ann, jeez. Not for having…I mean…" He lifted one shoulder. "I'm sorry I didn't recognize you. I know it sounds lame, but I kinda had a feeling."

"It doesn't matter. It's interesting, really. I didn't realize how much difference it made, losing a few pounds, changing a few things. Good to know." She took the picture back. "There were so many pretty women there that night, Zach. I've often wondered why you picked me."

"Picked you?" He remembered asking her to dance. Not *asking,* exactly. Taking her by the hand and leading her onto the dance floor—a smooth move, one he'd made often. *Charitable* wasn't the word he would have used. He liked all shapes, sizes and types of women, and he enjoyed showing them a good time. "How did we end up?"

"You fell asleep, and I left."

"After…"

"After we had sex, yes."

"Damn." Not for the *having sex* part, but for the *how did we end up?* and the *falling asleep* part.

"That's what *I* said." She tucked the picture back into the little book. "What I thought, anyway. I left quietly." She looked up smiling. "Imagine my surprise finding you on my porch the other night, still sleeping."

"*Ripped* Van Winkle." He wagged his head slowly.

"That's a sad tale, Annie. For a minute there I thought you'd seen me at my best."

"I'm sure I did. I don't know much about rodeo, but I knew I was watching something special. Not only that, but you rode well. I had Sally there to explain all the fine points."

"Can't just hang on till you hear the buzzer anymore. These days you gotta have fine points. They stick that microphone in your face, you gotta have a story."

"You had that."

"Aw, jeez. Now I gotta live up to God knows what I said while I'm tryin' to live down what I did. You're holdin' all the cards here. You and God."

She patted his thigh. "You assume we're playing. I don't know about God, but I've moved on. I don't even know why I told you."

"I'm glad you did. New deal, okay? Forget that night." Bad idea. He erased it from the air with a wave of his hand. "Okay, I'll try to remember. You try to forget." He sighed. "I never had much to say when they stuck the microphone in my face. Stick a bottle in my face, and pretty soon I'm saying any fool thing comes into my head. I don't drink much these days."

"You're on a lot of medication."

"I'm not *on*..." He glanced away. "I don't use it much. Not anymore."

"I'm glad you're here, Zach." She laid her hand on his thigh again. No patting this time. "Really. It's good to see you again. I hope you can stay longer than a week."

"You must not be counting the days."

"Aren't you?"

"Mainly when the phrase *overstaying your welcome* comes to mind. At least now I know why I make you uncomfortable. I thought it was because I'm just so damned irresistible."

She laughed. "I've gotten much better at resisting."

"Game on."

"Oh, grow up." She smacked his thigh.

"Damn. I was just beginning to feel like a kid again, what with Christmas coming and all." He caught her hand first, then her gaze. "If you need me, I can stay awhile."

"You're welcome here."

Welcome was something. Enough to hold him, at least for now.

Chapter Six

Hoolie liked to make breakfast, especially on Saturday mornings. Ann remembered the first time, not long after her mother's death, when she'd complained about cold cereal, and Hoolie had made "flaps." She'd been skeptical, but he'd turned out to be a skilled flap flipper, no spatula required. Hoolie donned the white bib apron less often these days, but padding into a daybreak-lit kitchen to find him warming up the cast-iron skillet was the best morning greeting Ann could imagine, and she still cheered for him on the first flip.

"Is that all it takes?"

Ann turned toward the voice coming from the mudroom. An armload of firewood clattered to the floor, and Zach grinned at her. "Mornin'."

Ann nodded impassively, which wasn't easy. She was breathing the scent of hot pancakes and feasting her eyes on a delicious-looking man. His face was radiant, tinted by cold-morning chores, and his eyes gleamed as though he had a secret, and, boy, wouldn't she like to know what it was.

"That's all I get?" He imitated her nod. "All Hoolie did was flip a pancake."

"But it fell neatly back into the pan," she pointed out. "You have a ways to go."

Cocking her a gloved finger, Zach opened the back door and let Kevin in with another armload of split firewood. "Let me help you with that, my man." He closed the door and started stacking Kevin's wood directly into the rack. "I'm catchin' hell for making a mess on the floor."

"Already?" The boy added the last two logs to the pile. "Morning, Miss Drexler. I'll stack the rest, Zach." He raised his voice. "Sure smells good in there, Hoolie."

Zach slipped Ann a sly wink as he shrugged his jacket off. "Am I there yet, Miss Drexler?"

"Very close."

"I don't work for cigars," he told her as he helped himself to coffee. "Just so we're clear when the time comes."

"Hoo-wee!" Sally exclaimed as she rounded the corner into the kitchen. "I feel the power. I hear the crackle." She was on her feet and grinning from one face to another. "Good morning, all. There's electricity in the air. How exciting!"

"Purely static," Ann said.

"And she's givin' it to me by the mouthful," Zach teased. "Can I get you some coffee, Sally?"

"Who's up for some ridin' today?" Hoolie proposed as he delivered a platter of golden-brown pancakes to the table. "We gotta move the cows in closer. Weather's comin' in tomorrow."

"I watched the weather forecast last night." Sally parked her cane in the corner nearest the table and claimed a chair. "The Ken doll promised clear skies for the next three days."

"You believe that weatherman's plastic face or my arthritic knees, big sister? I'm sayin' snow, and plenty of it."

Zach's knee gave a loud crack as he joined Sally at the table. "Is that what I'm feelin'?"

"You got it, too?" Hoolie asked. "'Course you do. You're a cowboy. A little young yet, but you've been pushin' extra hard. Did I tell you I used to ride bareback? Not professional. Just backyard stuff."

"Cowboy knees, huh?" Zach poured on the syrup and then handed it to Kevin. "Guess that's the price of the cowboy ass." He gave Ann a passing glance as he licked his forefinger. "Can we *make* it snow, or just forecast it? I was thinkin' of getting myself some plastic. Maybe I'll put it in my face instead of my knee and become a weatherman."

"Question is, can we make it quit?" Hoolie exchanged the empty pancake platter for a full one. "Answer is no, which is why we're gonna saddle up soon as we finish breakfast. What these girls don't know is us cowboys, we put in half a day's work before they even put on their socks. So we already know it's cold enough out there to shrivel rocks. Right, boys?"

Smiling, Zach glanced at Kevin, who rolled his eyes. "A little cowboy poetry," Zach said.

So this was it, Zach thought as he rousted a pair of recalcitrant cows out of a clutch of buffalo berry bushes. This was a real cowboy's job. He'd taken part in almost every standard rodeo event at one time or another, was a decent steer wrestler and a fair roping hand, but he couldn't say he'd seriously worked cattle without being timed, scored or judged. It would have been an eye-opener if the Dakota sky hadn't been so unrelentingly clear and its cold, white sun so bright. Sunglasses would have been nice. He was going to kiss Ann when he got back to the house for stealing his Stetson and making him wear her father's wool cap. He hadn't worn earflaps since he was about ten. He was damn glad to be wearing them now.

Hoolie was wearing them, too, and Kevin sported a stocking cap. *No self-respecting cowboy,* Zach thought, and then he chuckled. His mantra. Back in the day, rodeo cowboys were required to wear cowboy hats and long sleeves. Boots, chaps and jeans were optional. Nowadays the protective gear made them look like a damn football team. Zach drew the line at the helmet with the face guard. The protective vest was okay, especially after he'd fractured a couple of ribs, but not that silly helmet. *No self-respecting cowboy…*

Hoolie had the herd moving steadily through the draw. Now there was a real cowboy, Zach thought with a stiff-lipped, squint-eyed smile. Headgear notwithstanding. The man made the clothes. A guy could learn a lot from Hoolie.

Given the time.

"Somebody's gotta go back for the one that got away," Hoolie told his two drovers as they added Zach's strays to the herd. "Old Ball Bustin' Betty, I call her. Always givin' me trouble."

"I gotta take a leak," Kevin said.

"Careful," Hoolie warned as the boy dismounted. "Don't forget how cold it is."

Zach chuckled. "I'll go after her. I think I saw which way she went."

"Try the opposite direction. That's probably where she ended up."

Hoolie was right. Zach would have saved himself some time if he'd listened. By the time he had Betty headed for home he had a few more names for her. Fingers frozen, toes numb, knee killing him, Zach had no qualms about pushing the hefty cow hard, using the fence to keep her in line. She finally stopped trying to turn back, and gave in to the pace he set. Had to give the mustang credit—wasn't even breathing hard. He ran the cow through the gate Hoolie had left open for him. The rest of the herd had already bellied up to the hay feeder. Hoolie was on the ground, and Kevin was nearby, holding their horses. Hoolie waved. Zach grinned, waved back, reined in and watched Betty put a little distance between her big brown butt and his proven cow pony before she stopped dead.

And then she dropped.

Zach looked up at Hoolie, who only had eyes for Betty. He hadn't been waving to welcome them home.

Betty had dropped dead.

Zach swung down from the saddle and hit the ground on numb toes. By the time he stood over the carcass, he was numb all over. Disbelief had displaced the cold.

"Overheated." Hoolie's boot heels dragged to a halt. Out of the corner of his eye Zach could see a scuffed toe, but the sightless eye on the ground kept him riveted. The four-beat approach of another horse moved little, changed nothing. Hoolie gave him another moment before asking, "How far did you run her?"

He didn't know. He knew one thing: he was looking at a dead cow.

"She kept trying to turn back on me," he said. "Once I got her going in the right direction, I kept her going at a good clip so she wouldn't get any second thoughts."

"Overheated."

The word made no more sense to Zach the second time. He looked at Hoolie, said the obvious because it was all that came to mind. "It's cold as hell."

"Yep. Cold on the outside, hot on the inside." Hoolie clapped a hand on Zach's back. "What we have here is hell frozen over."

"I'll be damned."

"Not without me." Hoolie gave another reassuring tap before letting his hand slide away. "I should've had a second thought. You're a rodeo cowboy. That's got nothin' to do with cows." He turned and raised his arm to block the sun. "Bulls, calves, steers, but no cows," he told Kevin, who sat silently in the saddle.

"I gotta get me a helmet," Zach muttered. "Can we butcher her?"

"Meat's no good. It's like blood-soaked sponge. Cows are touchy that way, you run 'em long and hard."

"Crap."

"That about sums up what's left," Hoolie said.

"It happens," Kevin said.

Hoolie nodded. "We don't have to say anything about this today."

"Forget *we*." Zach looked from one grim face to the other. "This is all mine."

"See there?" Hoolie instructed Kevin. "That's how you cowboy up."

"Don't forget the rules," Kevin reminded Zach.

"Watch me." Zach started toward the barn, leading his horse.

"You need backup?"

"This is gonna be an unrehearsed solo." Zach turned back to his companions even as he kept walking. "Live and open to the public."

They found Ann sitting at the kitchen table working on school papers. A little white teapot stood beside a flowered cup and saucer near her right hand, and an array of books was lined up on the left. Cap in hand, Zach felt like a schoolboy. He got rid of the cap.

She looked up from her papers and watched them file

in. Hoolie said he was dying for coffee. Kevin hung back in the mudroom doorway. Zach pulled a chair away from the table and sat down. She glanced left and right, taking each of his cohorts in, before giving him the *what's-up* look.

"We just brought the cows in. Everything went fine, except...I killed Betty."

Ann did a double take. "Betty who?"

"Betty the cow. Nice big Hereford."

"Stubborn as hell," Hoolie put in as he poured water into the Mr. Coffee.

"I ran her to death." Still a little dazed, Zach shook his head. "She didn't wanna hang with the rest of the herd, so I had to bring her in separate. I pushed her too hard. Soon as she stopped, right out here, she...she just dropped dead. Damnedest thing I ever saw." He drew a deep breath and blew it out. "I don't know if I told you, I haven't worked cows all that much."

"So..." Ann glanced past Zach in search of her... foreman? "We have a dead cow?"

"Look, I'm really sorry," Zach put in quickly, eager to keep the spotlight where it belonged. "I'll take care of the carcass, of course. Hoolie says the meat's no good. And I'll pay for her, whatever you say. You probably lost a calf to boot."

"Betty was open," Hoolie reported from the other side of the kitchen. "Plus, she was ornery."

"She wasn't really running that fast." Kevin was still hanging in the doorway.

"My lawyers. Cowboy dream team." Zach couldn't

help smiling a little even though his face was probably flaming. "They're the cowboys. I'm just a stunt man. I'm really sorry."

Ann glanced at Hoolie again. "I didn't know the cows had names."

"Not all of 'em do. Just mainly the ornery ones."

"And she sure was that," Kevin offered.

"Well…" Ann stared at her papers for a moment, clicked her pen, laid it down, and finally gave Zach her full attention. "We lose one or two a year," she said. "Sometimes more. That's part of the business. Clearly, this was an accident."

"Stupid." Zach looked her in the eye and shook his head. "No excuse for it."

"That's his rule number two," Kevin chimed in for Ann's information, Zach's benefit. "No excuses."

"Most people don't know this," Hoolie said as he claimed a post at Zach's elbow, "but cows are kinda like dogs. No sweat glands. They drool and slobber, but they don't sweat. A lotta cowboys these days, they know more about horses. Now, horses, they sweat." He laid a hand on Zach's shoulder. "And so do cowboys."

"Better than drooling," Kevin quipped.

"Guess I shoulda done this in private." The last thing Zach wanted to do was smile. He tried to stay focused. "We got a dead cow outside, and it's my fault. I want to tell Sally myself, if you'll just let me know when she's—"

"She's all ears right now." Sally made her appearance without benefit of wheels or cane. Zach jumped up to offer his chair, but she waved him down and braced her hands on the back of an empty one. "I feel like a kid these days. If it wasn't for eavesdropping I'd be left out of everything."

The look in Ann's eyes as she watched her sister slid over Zach like a warm breeze. He felt the beauty of it, and he wanted more. He wanted some for himself.

"I thought you were resting," Ann said.

"I'm always resting. I need more activity. Can't hardly remember whether I sweat or drool."

Zach couldn't bring himself to laugh along with everyone else. He felt sick. That poor, dumb animal had tried to save herself from him, and he'd driven her to her death. Her legs had caved in under her like four dry twigs.

Hoolie must have read his mind. "Nobody saw it comin'," he said. "I've seen it happen before. Coulda said something. Didn't. You live and learn. Right, boy?"

Zach stiffened, glanced askance and realized Hoolie was looking at Kevin. He drew a deep breath. He knew all about *live and learn*. Yeah, he was embarrassed about what he'd done, but more than that, he was haunted by the image of a creature in pain. All he would have had to do was give her time, which was one of the few things he had to spare.

He gave Kevin half a smile. "Some mistakes cost more than others."

"It ain't all bad. Coyotes got pups to feed." Kevin abandoned the doorway and joined the circle around the kitchen table. "I'll help you, Zach. Maybe we can put her on the hill behind the shelter belt. What do you think, Hoolie?"

"I'll rig up the tractor."

Hoolie's joints had gotten ahead of themselves in forecasting snowfall for the next day, but timing was a minor detail. If Zach had learned anything by living, it was that pain gave all kinds of warnings. Live with it, learn from it, make preparations. Once Betty had been delivered to those in need—Kevin's observation—Zach moved on. One misstep didn't put him on the bench, out in the cold. He wouldn't be able to pay for the cow until he could get back to doing what he was good at, but he had other ideas, and he had a team ready to help him make short work of the first one on his list. And when it was finished, the whole team—shoulder to shoulder—headed for the house. They hung their coats, scraped their boots and searched for the two people they most wanted to please.

"We've got something to show you girls," Hoolie announced as they threaded around the bottom of the stairs and down the hallway.

"And it's wicked cool," Kevin piped up.

"And we're just in time." Zach reached Sally's open bedroom door first and found the women poring over some chart on the computer screen. "Because it's about to get wicked cold."

"We're going outside?" Ann gave Sally a solicitous look. "Are you—"

Weariness melted from Sally's face. "Damn right, I am. *Wicked* rules. It's what I live for."

The sky's heavy burden hung so low that Zach itched to reach up and poke a hole in the sack just to see what would come out. He might be sorry later, but the tension begged to be busted wide open, and busting—that exquisite instant when all hell broke loose and heaven was on the line—was irresistible. If he only had the reach.

Hell, maybe he did. Leading his little procession in one barn door and out the other, he was feeling that good.

"You moved the water tank?" Ann asked.

"We remodeled the water tank," Zach said as he halted at the corner of the building and gestured expansively.

"Zach designed it," Kevin said. "Hoolie came up with all the materials."

Zach's gesturing hand landed on the boy's shoulder. "Every inch between the tank and the box is insulated, thanks to Kevin's hard work."

"We wanted to get it done today, but we didn't take shortcuts. It's solid." Kevin fairly skipped around the newly boxed-in tank toward the south side. "And you'll love this part, Miss Drexler." He ran his hand over the glass facing affixed to the wooden surround. "Passive solar energy. I got *passive* right on the vocabulary test after we talked about passive solar energy in class. Like you said, wave of the future."

"And the future is now," Ann recited with a smile.

"Plus, we used stuff you already had. Not recycled, but re*purposed*. Like you said."

"Sounds like quite a lesson," Zach said.

"The interesting stuff sinks in," said Kevin. "Right, Hoolie?"

"Sure looks like it."

Zach moved behind Ann, put his hands on her shoulders and steered her toward a different view. "It wasn't easy, but we moved it around for maximum southern exposure. And this part was Kevin's idea." He pointed out the sturdy wire fence that created a no-cow zone. "The glass is protected from the stock, plus you've got better windbreak on the north side from the barn."

"Ingenious." Ann waved her sister over. "Sally, meet the Three Wise Men."

Hoolie escorted Sally, and they formed a half circle around the new construction, the three men grinning as though they'd been decorated with medals.

"I was trying to work a new tank heater into the budget, but now…" Sally's whole face lit up. "Now I feel better about bidding on that lease." She quickly added, "Don't worry, Annie. If our neighbor has anything to say about it, we probably won't get it. But if we do—" she hugged Hoolie's arm "—the Three Wise Men are working for us now."

"They were visitors," Ann reminded her.

"Visitors are a breath of fresh air," Sally said. "Neighbors can be a blast of halitosis."

Zach scowled. "Somebody who's not a horse lover? Sounds purely foul."

Sally nodded. "Hard to imagine, isn't it?"

"Damn tootin'," Hoolie chimed in, grinning.

"*Dan* Tutan." Ann gave Hoolie's shoulder a playful shove. "His name is Dan Tutan."

"Whoa, that's sad. Cursed by his own mama." But

Zach laughed. "There oughta be a sanctuary for kids with bad names."

"In my next life," Sally said. "In this one I'm all in for wild horses. Tutan can't use the land himself, but he filed a bogus complaint against us with the BLM. Says we aren't maintaining our fences and that the horses are getting into his pasture. Ultimately, he can't back it up, but he can muddy the waters for who knows how long."

"Meanwhile, the BLM is proposing to slaughter horses again," Ann said quietly.

"They're always *proposing*," Sally pointed out. "We get the word out, people protest, and proposals go back in the bottom drawer."

But Ann was worried. "They're talking about 30,000 head."

"Man, that's…" Zach shook his head, and they all stood in silence, images assaulting each horse-loving head.

"This is amazing," Ann said of their elaborate creation. "You guys could go into business making solar water tanks."

"Zach designed it," Kevin said again. "I bet he could get it copyrighted."

"*Patented,*" Zach corrected his new fan. "There's nothing new here. I put together different parts of other guys' ideas."

Ann turned, smiled up at him and surprised him by subtly slipping her arm around his back. "I think that's what most inventors do. And I think this is fabulous."

"Just for you, Miss Drexler." Zach smiled back. "Hope it works."

"Here she comes." Head tipped back, Hoolie directed all attention skyward. "The wicked witch from the north."

One white flake drifted past Zach's nose like a lacy little parachute. No wind. No real anger overhead, but neither was there any horizon. Heaven had gained weight and gone gray. It was slowly sagging down on them.

"The witch from the north was the good one. East and west were the wicked ones," Ann said. "But good things come from the east and west in Indian tradition. Right, Kevin?"

"I guess so."

"Good things come from all directions," Zach said. "Bad things, too. Sometimes both at once, you know? Both in the same package."

Ann's arm slid away. Easy come, easy go. "Is that Indian philosophy?" she asked Zach.

"Indian cowboy philosophy. To boot, we've got our own prayer." He lifted his eyes to the ominous heavens. *"God grant me the heart for hunting the bull, the head for throwing the bull, and the legs for getting the hell out of the way when the bull turns on me."*

"Is that for real, or did you just make that up?" Kevin wanted to know.

"Both." Zach slid Ann a flirty smile. "You gotta watch yourself around Indian cowboys, Miss Drexler."

Ann was an expert on watching herself when it came to men, but what she'd been watching lately was a strange bird who didn't seem to know when to get the hell off the wire. She ought to know better than to mix water with electricity, but there she was, rinsing dishes with one hand and taking them from hot-wired hands with the other. If she kept this up, she was in for a shock.

What would it feel like this time?

"You don't have to do this, you know. You earned your supper with that fabulous water tank upgrade."

"It's my excuse to hang around you." She glanced up at him, and he chuckled. "Don't look so scared. Last night was my first time hanging up decorations. Got me a hankerin' for hangin' with you."

She wasn't scared, and she was pretty sure he knew it. "I'll make coffee, and we'll hang in the living room, then. Enjoy the ambiance we created."

"Mmm. *Ambiance.* Sounds warm and sexy."

"As does anything French." She filled the glass carafe half-full. She was a half-full kind of girl. "How have you escaped decorating all these years? You never helped your mother decorate the store for the holidays?"

"As long as my brother was there to help out, I never had to." He slid the coffee can across the counter toward her and then hunkered down, elbows planted at the counter where she had a ninety-degree view of him. "By the time he left, there was no going back. I couldn't be housebroken."

"You're the baby." She paused in her coffee scooping to give him a teasing glance. "Don't look so scared. No one's dissing your manhood. I mean that in the nicest way." She lifted one shoulder. "One baby to another."

"Fair enough."

"Tell me about your brother. It's just the two of you, right?"

He nodded. "My dad died when I was eight, and my big brother took over. He was *the man*. Good at everything he does. Serious. Responsible. I tried to be just like him, but Sam I am *not*. So I just tagged along, you know, trying to match his stride and step in his tracks. Then all of a sudden he graduates from high school and decides to take off for the oil fields." He snapped his fingers. "Just like that. Be damned if I'll be his replacement on the baseball team or behind the counter at Allgood's Emporium. I've got better things to do. Let's see Sam Beaudry make the whistle on a rank bull."

He gave her a piece of a smile, which she returned with a side serving of empathy.

"Tell you about my brother," he offered. He had her ear, and he seemed interested in keeping it. "He's a good man. Best I know. He went to work in the oil fields to help Ma pay the bills and turn the store around. It was a struggle for a while there after we lost Dad. Sam was a Marine. Now he's the sheriff of Bear Root County. Dependable. Patient. He can bring in a stray without runnin' him to death."

"Having gone astray yourself?"

"Once or twice." He pushed away from the counter. "Call myself a cowboy, don't know a damn thing about cows. False advertising is what that is."

"No sweat glands," she said. "Who knew? Call myself a rancher." She opened a glass cupboard door and took down the sugar bowl. "Sally's the rancher in the family. I'm just doing what I can to help." She added two mugs. "Which is all you were trying to do, so don't be so hard on yourself."

"You'd like Sam. He'd never..."

"Forget a woman he'd gotten naked with?" Ann laughed. Solo. Was her remark cold, or just plain crude? Have it either or both ways, she told herself. He deserved it.

It didn't feel right, but she kept at it.

"We weren't naked," she said, eyes on pouring coffee, ears noting his silence. *Guess he's not that into my cheeky side.* She added a little kick by looking him in the eye as she handed him coffee. He'd been hit, but he was taking it like a man.

And she was feeling it like a woman.

"It was a long time ago, Zach, and it was one night." She touched his temple and reminded him, "Give it a rest."

"I just don't see it." He caught her hand, not to push it away, but to draw it to his chest. "It doesn't fit. How many one-night stands have you had? Ballpark? I'm guessing one."

"Isn't that enough? It wasn't good for me. Why do it again? It wasn't memorable." She took her hand back. "Secrets are just bothersome. Given the circumstances, I thought full disclosure was only fair."

"I can believe... How drunk was I?"

"I don't know. You were having a good time, and you invited me to join in. I was flattered. You were *the man.* Ordinarily I would've huddled in Sally's shadow, but that night she had business to attend to."

"And you went astray."

"That I did," she admitted as she reached for her coffee.

"And I came up short."

"That you did." She gave a tight smile. "I didn't even break a sweat."

"Give me another chance." His promising smile trumped her empty one. "I'll show you paces you didn't know you had."

She used the remaining wind in her sails to take her to the window. Snowflakes glistened as they darted through the yard light's beam. "It's really coming down out there. Hoolie's never far off in his predictions. He really should be…"

His barely audible footsteps belied his proximity, but she felt him at her back even before he laid hands on her shoulders.

She turned into his arms and lifted her face for the gentle kiss she'd also felt coming.

"What can I do for you, baby?" He lifted a wisp of hair from the side of her face and twirled it around his forefinger. "One baby to another. I feel like we're two sides of a coin."

"And I would be heads or…"

"The shiny side."

"Nice call."

Chapter Seven

By morning the snow had stopped falling, but Hoolie's joints were still forecasting round two of "the blizzard of the century." Given Hoolie's comment about recent winters, Zach figured the old man had the odds in his favor, and his repeated suggestion sure had power. It was brewing up a storm in Zach's hip, along with a few other abused parts.

Damn. He was too young to be comparing aches and pains with old men.

Zach lifted his mind over the matter of his weaker parts, forcing them to straighten up and move right as he headed for the corral to saddle up for his morning assignment. Never knew who might notice his cowboy ass from the kitchen window. Maybe he didn't know much about cows, but he knew women. They appreciated a tightly packed trunk.

Ann Drexler's appreciation would be sweet. He'd take it any way she cared to offer it. If she didn't care, he couldn't really blame her. But he'd pretty much decided to keep trying, at least for the duration. He'd made points with her on the water tank, and with the break in the weather, he had a chance to try for a few more. Maybe he was short on cow competency, but he'd developed considerable horse sense. If nothing else, he knew a rank horse from a biddable one.

And he valued both, which was probably why Hoolie wanted him to check out a group of two- and three-year-olds before he brought the "geriatrics" in closer and released the young horses into the hills for the winter. The old man figured Zach might see some he liked, and he'd start getting ideas. They seemed to be popping into his head right and left lately.

What did they call it when one body part started to go downhill and another kicked in? *Compensation.* He laughed as he adjusted the cheek strap on his bridle, scratched his mount's neck, and imagined himself growing a big head.

He was about to take off when a fancy pickup pulled into the yard and a stout man wearing a down-filled parka, sunglasses and a broad-brimmed tan Stetson emerged. Zach led the saddled bay across the yard and greeted the man with the traditional Western nod.

"Came to talk to somebody about the horses," the man announced.

"What's up?" Zach pulled off a glove and stuck out his hand. "Zach Beaudry. I'm workin' for the Drexlers."

"Beaudry? The bull rider?" The handshake turned vigorous. "Dan Tutan. Big rodeo fan. My place is just north of the Double D."

"How're the roads?"

"Could be worse. My four-wheel drive sits pretty high off the ground, so I didn't have any trouble." The ruddy-faced Tutan adjusted his glasses and grinned. "Hell, I saw you in Vegas a few years back. You won the go-round on a rank bull. A real spinner." He took a hands-on-hips stance and surveyed the outbuildings as though they were new to him. "You're *working* here?"

"That's right."

"Don't let 'em pay you in horses. Only thing around here that ain't past its prime is the younger sister."

Take it easy. Find out what he wants.

Zach stuck his hand back in his glove. "I'm a big fan of wild horses."

Tutan nodded. "Doin' a little charity work, are you?"

"Mainly I do the dirty work." The big bay snorted and scraped a trough in the snow. Zach scratched the horse's cheek. "So what can I do for you, Dan?"

"I'm afraid some of your *endangered* mustangs are endangering my hay. There's some fence down this morning that was just fine two days ago."

"How do you know it was horses?"

"I spotted about a dozen of them hangin' out in that area last week." The man turned ninety degrees and gazed westward. "The way I understood, you're supposed to be runnin' 'em up in the hills west of my place. That's where this so-called sanctuary was supposed to be."

"You're sure the horses you saw were mustangs?"

"Yep." He turned to Zach again. "Got no use for horses myself, but I know them wild ones when I see 'em. Canners. Those girls could make a nice living making dog food. Put up a factory, hire some unemployed Indians."

"They did that."

"Yeah, do us all a favor, including the dogs. Now there's a useful..." Tutan did a double take. "Did what?"

"Hired a couple of unemployed Indians." Zach gave a cold grin. "Maybe they could be canned, too."

Needlessly adjusting his glasses, Tutan shifted his stance, still eyeing Zach as though he didn't quite know what to make of him. "'Course, they're all protected now, aren't they? Endangered species. But so's my hay. Tell Hoolie if I drive out there and find road apples and broken bales, I'm goin' to court this time. I never wanted this refuge for broken-down mustangs in my backyard."

"You seem to be a pretty unhappy man. You think goin' to court might change that somehow?"

Tutan's mouth formed a thin, tight line. Now he knew.

"I been to court a few times." He folded his arms around the barrel that passed for a torso. "Win or lose, I ain't unhappy. I know my rights, and I take great pleasure in exercisin' 'em."

"It's kinda fun to see just how far you can push a

guy." Zach nodded consideringly. "Until it isn't. See, I know dirty work. I've been to court. And I take great pleasure in mopping up the courtroom floor with bitter people." He tapped the man's upper arm with the back of his gloved hand. "So how about it? A little one-on-one?"

"I got no beef with you. All I want is—"

"—my ass in a can. Bring it on."

Tutan eyed him, frowning, trying to determine his pedigree without coming out and asking. Zach enjoyed this game. He'd played it many times.

Tutan settled on an approach. "You're not from around here."

"And you're damn tootin'. But that don't mean I ain't Indian."

"Well, I was just kiddin' about…" The neighbor took a step back, unfolding his arms, easing up. "Look, I didn't mean anything by what I said. It's hard to make a living in the cattle business these days. Grass is dry. Hay's goin' for top dollar. What the hell do those girls want with all them worthless wild horses? Their day is over, man."

"Whose?"

"The mustangs. Hell, the Drexlers. When their dad died, they shoulda sold out."

"You made an offer?"

"Damn right. Good one, too."

"They say every man has his price." Zach clucked tongue in cheek. "Too bad women aren't that simple."

"Why don't I go in the house and—"

Zach and the bay stood in the man's way.

"Why don't you turn your monster truck around and go home? I'll go have a look. If the mustangs broke your fence down, I'll fix it. I'll do the dirty work. Like I said, that's what I'm here for."

Zach enjoyed watching the fancy pickup retrace its tracks in the snow. He reached to the saddle horn and felt something brush against the back of his legs. He turned and was treated to a lolling-tongued canine smile.

He looked around for Kevin as he patted the black-and-white shepherd's head. "What do you think of the neighbor, Baby? Haven't you ever felt like just tearin' off one of those prickly jowels?" The dog whined. "Yeah, you're right. Probably taste like something the cat dragged in. If I have to rip his face off, I won't call you for supper." He chuckled as he headed for the barn on a pissing-contest-winner's high, the dog trotting close to his side, horse plodding along on the other. If Kevin had finished up in the barn, they could ride together.

"Baby, baby, ba-by," Zach sang softly. "Who named you, Baby? Bet I can guess. She's got a thing about babies." A thought pitched him a notch higher—maybe she really was watching from the kitchen. And maybe she'd seen him send Damn Tootin' down the road with his tail tucked between his legs. And maybe she was thinking to herself, maybe even singing…

"Baby, baby, ba-by."

* * *

"I'd rather talk to him myself," Ann told Zach hours later.

Her cool tone pushed the mute button on the jaunty tune his mind's ear had played for him whenever Kevin had run out of personal questions and teenage would-be shockers. Damn. He'd thawed out in the shower, scrubbed down and cleaned up while he counted the minutes to the one when he would join her at the table where she had her school papers all spread out. He'd been picturing his welcome. She'd give him a smile that looked as sweet as the kitchen smelled, listen to his report for the day and ask him just what he thought of it all. And then—just to let him know that one mistake did not an idiot make—she'd take his opinion for gospel.

Dream on, Beaudry.

"Would you like coffee?" He shook his head. "How about tea? I'm having some. I really appreciate…but the thing is, Zach, I have no trouble dealing with…what did you call him?"

"A knothead." He straddled a chair.

"To his face?"

"Of course not. I'm talkin' to *your* face. I'm giving you a cleaned-up version." He noticed her feet, covered in fuzzy red socks and propped up on the seat of another kitchen chair, and he smiled. "Just kidding. I didn't call him anything to his face. And I only told him one little white lie." He lifted one shoulder. "I've never been to court."

"My neighbor has."

"So he said."

"Many times. He took Hoolie to small-claims court over damage he claimed Hoolie did to his pickup."

"Accident?"

"Hoolie helped the Tutan boy when he had some engine trouble. Turned out the boy wasn't supposed to be driving the thing, and Dan claimed that Hoolie did something that caused further damage to the pickup, like, weeks later. The man enjoys…"

"Sucking people dry?" Zach shook his head. "You gotta figure a greedy bastard like that will keep on suckin' till he explodes. You wanna keep your distance."

"I want you and Hoolie to keep your distance and let me deal with him. I don't intend to cede any more ground to Dan Tutan, and I'd appreciate it if you guys wouldn't, either."

"I didn't give him anything."

"Satisfaction?"

"Hell, no. I'm way ahead of him there."

"Halfway to Texas," she said as she moved a test paper from one stack to another. "Sally and I have to live with him. Close, anyway—closer than we'd like— so please let me deal with him."

"I said I'd have a look at his fence. If it was horses, I'll fix it."

"I can send Hoolie to fix it, regardless."

"No, you can't. Not that he wouldn't do it, but you know you can't ask that of him after what you just told me." She scowled at him, but he wasn't backing down. "Damn Tootin's done nothing to me, and he ain't about to. You let me take care of this for you. I need to earn my keep." She opened her mouth, but he cut her off. "I promise not to run your neighbor to ground."

"I'm managing this operation," Ann said quietly. "My sister and I. There can be no doubt that we're in charge."

"You see any doubt on this face? I'm just tryin' to help out."

"I mean, outside these walls." Her gesture took in two of them. "The Double D has been here as long as anyone around here remembers, but this sanctuary survives day to day. I'm holding the vultures off with smoke and mirrors. I don't want them to start thinking I'm nothing but a scarecrow."

He laid his hand over hers. "It don't hurt to fire off a warning shot once in a while."

"Do what you and Hoolie think best," she said quietly. "Tutan'll be back with a new complaint next week."

"I'll be ready," he said, adding quickly, "to back your play. You're in charge." He squeezed her hand. "Hey. Almost forgot. Hoolie got my pickup runnin'."

"Great." She didn't sound too enthusiastic.

"So I could leave anytime you want me to."

"I don't want…" She glanced away. "I don't know what your schedule is, but you're welcome to stay as long as you want to."

Her cheeks were turning pink. *She was serious.*

"Hoolie says there's a dance at the VFW tonight," Zach said. "Complete with eggnog and mistletoe, he says. You wanna go?"

"What if it snows?"

"What if it doesn't?"

Again she glanced away. "I don't think so."

"I'm a pretty good dancer," he prodded.

"I know." She gave a perfunctory smile. "I have things to do."

"Me, too." He pushed off the back of the chair, stood up, then leaned down close to her. "You know what? I'm beginning to think you're putting me on. I don't believe we ever ma—" She started gathering up her papers, rustling, drowning him out until he slapped his hand down on the table and stilled the distraction. "I don't believe we ever made it together. It's some kind of joke you're playing on me. Messin' with my head, for whatever reason." He removed his hand, calming himself. "You don't wanna go out with me, fine."

"I don't go to the VFW," she said quietly. She lifted her eyes to meet his. "It's nothing personal, Zach. You don't have to get mad."

"I'm not mad." *So back off, Beaudry. Go kick up your heels. You keep this up, you'll be kicking your...* "For the record, I asked you personally, and you turned me down. *Personally.*"

"Not you," she whispered. She squared her shoulders and drew a deep breath. "*Parties.* Bars, dances, weddings, funerals, receptions. I don't like the noise, don't like the smell, the taste, the crowd, don't dance, can't think of anything to say, don't like…" She shook her head. "It's not *you*. I'm just no good at parties."

He smiled sympathetically. "Give me a chance to prove you wrong."

"You'll be so busy being good at it yourself, you won't notice how hopeless I am. And I'll say, *told ya.* And you'll say, *you couldn't prove it by me.*"

"Sounds like you already made that go-round."

"Once or twice," she said.

"Let me know when you're ready to try for the third-time charm. All you have to do is reach out, girl." He rapped his knuckles on the table. "I promised Hoolie I'd go."

"I'll see you when I see you," she said airily. "Be safe."

He smiled as he reached for his black Stetson.

"And have fun."

Adjusting his hat, he paused to make one more come-on—dancing eyes, a silent tip of his head—but she stood firm, hardly a trace of regret in her smile.

Ann had learned the value of keeping a lid on regrets. Maybe they didn't die off completely in the dark, but they atrophied, given time. The trick was to move on to something else. Holiday baking was a cheerful choice. As soon as she heard the roar of a truck carrying men in search of excitement, Ann put away her papers and pulled out her pans. She craved the feel of granulated sugar under her fingernails, the sound of table knives cutting butter into flour, the taste of chocolate scraped from the side of a mixing bowl. Let them have their tedious saloon.

"Do I smell sugar cookies?" Sally followed her nose into the kitchen, looking perkier than she had in weeks. "It seems awfully quiet around here."

"We're missing the holiday bash at the VFW."

"All of us?"

"You and I are missing it." Ann slipped the tip of an unfrosted Christmas tree into her sister's mouth. "And Kevin, presumably. His mother came to get him for a family gathering."

"Why are we missing it?" Sally sucked a fallen crumb from her forefinger. "Aren't we invited?"

"We are, but I didn't think you were up to it." Ann ate the bottom half of the cookie. "And I'm certainly not."

"What's wrong? Are you *sick?* You mean there were two cowboys ready to take us dancing, and you turned them down without asking me?"

"Sally…"

"Don't *Sally* me. You know better." She glanced at the cluttered counter and the red oven light. "We're going."

"It's going to start snowing again." Ann looked out the window. The yard was dark and still. "Any minute now."

Sally took another cookie. "We're going, Annie."

"I'll drop you off."

"What will people think, you dropping your pitiful sister off in front of the VFW and driving away?" Sally linked her arm with Ann's. "Nope, *we* are going to the party."

"Pitiful my… You know how I feel about—"

"This is what I want for Christmas, Annie. Just this." For emphasis she squeezed Ann's arm. "I want to go out for an hour or two. I want to see people I haven't seen in ages, listen to some music, carouse a little bit like we used to. Like *I* used to. You know I won't last long." Ann's exasperation turned to panic. "*Tonight,* Annie. I'm gonna live forever, but tonight I won't make last call. I'll be on my best behavior, and I won't push myself." She patted Ann's cheek. "Or you."

"You don't play fair."

"Of course not." Sally gave a saucy smile. "You know you want to, you big chicken. Zach asked you, and you were dying to go with him, but you turned him down automatically. You're a fat kid living in a skinny woman's body, Annie. Get over yourself. Take a chance."

"I've done that."

"Time to do it again. Are we going, or not?" The oven timer buzzed, and Ann tried to pull away, but Sally held tight. "Do I get my Christmas present, or not?"

"An hour."

Sally released her hold. "Starting when we get there."

"Less if it snows."

The band was pretty bad, but the dancers didn't seem to notice. After a few shots, most of them required little more from the music than some kind of tempo. They hopped, skipped and spun around the dance floor like a flock of mating grouse. Unlike grouse, males and females in the VFW crowd were dressed alike in drab blue jeans and nondescript shirts. They didn't have to work as hard as birds. Any man on top of his biological and environmental game could easily pole vault into the catbird's seat. *So, look out, party people.* After a few more shots, Zach Beaudry would find the beat and take the leap. He'd knocked back a double, but the band still sounded pretty bad.

Hoolie had taken to the floor when two middle-aged sisters had attached themselves to his arms and become the wings for his chrysalis. They were dancing the Butterfly. It was the requisite set of Western dance songs Zach routinely sat out until Last Call loomed in close. Then he'd get crazy with the rest of the flock. But it was taking some doing tonight. His head was like a snow globe in a kid's hands—couldn't stop shaking up thoughts of Ann. And all of a sudden they seemed to be taking shape on the other side of the room. Between side-kicking threesomes, he could have sworn he'd glimpsed a lark among the grouse.

She glided across the floor unscathed and lighted on Hoolie, who nodded toward "the fort" Zach had offered to hold down. Suddenly the table and the two drinks Hoolie had ordered were as unimportant as the server shouting the tally in his ear. He dropped Hoolie's money on her tray and walked away from the change. That band sounded pretty damn good.

"Just in time." Zach tipped the brim of his hat and offered Sally his right elbow and Ann his left. "This number takes three."

"Watch out for your knee," Ann warned.

He grinned. "*You* watch out for my knee."

Sally's cane kept the other twirling butterfliers from crashing into them. She dropped off the three-link chain as Hoolie met them at the table and the music downshifted for a slow dance.

Zach took Ann in his arms, buried his nose in her hair and rocked her side to side. "Sweet heaven, woman, you smell delicious. Like my mother's kitchen at Christmastime."

"Sugar cookies." She looked up smiling. "You can buy the scent in a spray can."

He inhaled deeply. "No, this is the real thing. I've got my arms full of Christmas cookies. You packed 'em all up in round tins painted with winter scenes."

"Not all," she promised. "There's a plate for the boys and a plate for Santa Claus."

"What boys?"

"Hoolie and Kevin." Her eyes twinkled, suggesting a worthwhile wait. "And you."

One in three wasn't good enough. He wanted the whole plate.

"I guess you've never had a shortage of boys around the place, huh? Real cowboys?"

"Does anyone know what that is anymore? You're their idea of a real cowboy. Crisscrossing the country-side from one rodeo to another—Hoolie and Kevin would love to have your life."

He pressed his cheek against hers. "What part could I trade them for their share of the cookies?"

"All I know is, the cookies are real."

"So's my cowboy two-step."

"You're a very good dancer," she quipped *Rain Man* style.

"And you're way too cool, woman." He held her close. "But I'm gonna warm you up."

"Really."

"Look up." He had danced her under a mistletoe ball suspended from a dim light fixture, and lifting her gaze had put her sweet lips in perfect position for a quick kiss.

Somebody behind him gave a wolf whistle, and he smiled against her mouth as he pivoted her in an exuberant circle.

Ann matched him, kiss for kiss, smile for smile, and step for step. She was on top of the world, but it felt like heaven. Something like the night they'd met—right at the start, when he'd plucked her off a knotty pine wall and moved her to the music—but with a safety net of her own making. And she felt good about that.

She felt good about getting Sally out of the house. She was due a round of remission, and maybe a night out would bring it on. People were thrilled to see her, and Ann would have been perfectly happy to be her sister's bodyguard if Hoolie hadn't claimed the job for himself. But that left Ann without purpose. No choice but to join the party, or be a pooper. With Zach dancing on her turf, she'd be damned if she would go the pooper route. She wasn't about to change her mind about the smoke or the booze or the noise, but with a partner like Zach Beaudry, anybody could dance.

Ann's heart fell when Sally gave the high sign. She was having too much fun. But Sally surprised her with the news that Hoolie would be taking her home.

"No way," Ann shouted over the din. "It's Hoolie's night off, and I'm…I'm ready to go."

Sally waved off the offer. "You kids are having a good time. We're tired. Right, Hoolie?"

"You got that right."

"I called the Thunder Shields," Sally said. "Kevin's ready to go, so we're gonna pick him up and get home while the gettin's still good. We've got two vehicles. We need two designated drivers. We're good on our end. You two figure it out." She winked at Zach. "You really *can* party, Annie. Don't stop now."

Ann smiled at Zach. "Maybe one more dance."

Or two. Or four. He taught her steps she didn't know, moves she'd never cared to try. She did now. But by the time they bundled up and got out of the VFW, the gettin' was no longer good. Enough snow had fallen to make it worth the wind's while to start throwing its weight around.

Zach unlocked his pickup, fired up the engine, pulled the scraper out from under the seat and started cleaning off the windshield. Ann was right behind him.

"I turned the heat on," he said, nodding toward the passenger's side.

"I'm driving."

"Hey, honey, I'm good to go," he shouted jovially. "I been takin' it real easy, in case you didn't notice."

"And you're good to *co*. As in copilot." She patted his arm and reiterated, "I'm a very good driver."

He scowled, but she wasn't backing down, so he leaned over and peered into the windshield. "What do you think, Zel? Should we trust her?" He laughed. "Better her than me, you say? Damn females."

It was the kind of driving nobody enjoyed, but every South Dakotan had to do from time to time, and Ann was no exception. More assault than storm, the weather bore down on the prairie moonscape as though blasted from a cannon. Snow washed through the air horizontally, and wind squabbled with windshield wipers over where it would land. Zach's pickup handled well, but Ann wished she were driving a more familiar vehicle. Zelda had her idiosyncrasies—the play in her steering, the inefficiency of her wiper blades—but the real worry was the risk of doing her damage. Thanks to Zach, Ann felt as though she were taking a piggyback ride on the man's dearest friend.

While he slept through it all.

"Angel Annie."

Maybe not. But he'd reclined his seat, and he'd been remarkably quiet. She risked a quick glance and snatched a modicum of comfort from the warmth in his eyes.

"Figured you didn't need me pressin' my nose to the glass," he explained. "But I'm here for you, Captain. You need me to talk, or keep quiet?"

"Talk is good." Maybe she'd learn something.

"Okay." He hiked his seat back up. "Why don't you want me to call you Annie?"

"Annie reminds me of an orphan. Or a gunslinger."

"Annie Oakley wasn't a gunslinger. She was a terrific marksman. Little Sure Shot, the Indians called her."

"Sitting Bull called her that." She knew her South Dakota history. "Old diminutives die hard," she said as she wrestled with the steering wheel over a road turned washboard. "Your pickup bucks."

"Zelda loves pillow drifts. She could eat 'em all night long."

"By the time we get home, she will have had her fill."

"You're doin' fine, baby." She cut her eyes at him and he smiled. "You, too, Annie."

"We're doing all the work, cowboy."

"Was that a smile?" He turned the defroster up a notch. "The night I stumbled onto your porch, I saw you through the window, decorating your Christmas tree. You looked like an angel that night, too."

She smiled at the snowflake onslaught on the windshield. "Keep talking."

"Did you order a white Christmas, Angel Annie? You might wanna ask your boss to turn it off now. I haven't even done my shopping yet. How the hell am I gonna do my Christmas shopping?" He shifted in the leather seat. "Okay. I'm not exactly a big Christmas shopper. But I always send my mother a big bunch of flowers. Once I even got it there on time. I think. There's no flower shop anywhere near Bear Root, so the little guy with the winged feet has to ride the bread truck." He touched her thigh. "What would you like for Christmas this year, little girl?"

Quivering inside—deep and low down—she gave a nervous chuckle. "More bars."

"A little competition for the VFW?"

"Heavens, no. One of those is plenty. I want cell bars."

"That's a tall order. I could probably come up with some handcuffs."

"I'm thinking much taller." She turned the windshield wipers up to top speed. "I want a tower. Cell phones are useless around here."

"Yeah, it's been a while since I had one."

"Zach?" She gripped the wheel and leaned forward. The onslaught had become whiteout. It was like being enclosed in an eggshell. "I'm scared. I can't tell whether we're still on the road."

"How far do we have to go?"

"About eight miles to the turnoff." Hard to imagine such a thing existed in an eggshell. "I think."

"You want me to drive? If I wasn't sober enough before, I sure am now."

"I'm afraid to stop. Ah!" She glimpsed something. A crack in the shell? Was this a good thing? "A little patch of yellow in the snow."

"Man trail," he declared, adding Hollywood Indian-style, "Good sign."

"Don't make me laugh! If we go in the ditch, they might not find us till spring." The sound of the door opening wasn't at all funny. "What are you doing?" He had his back to her, and she felt a draft.

"Cutting sign."

"What!"

"Don't worry. I ain't pissin' into *this* wind. A little to the left. I can see the shoulder. Left!"

She overcorrected. Zelda fishtailed, but Ann regained control.

"Let me get out and walk in front," Zach suggested.

"You'll freeze. Let me try…" Ann opened her door

and held it in close with her left hand. With her right hand on the wheel and eyes on the ground, she toed the accelerator until the wind whipped white snow feathers under the pickup and revealed a bit of yellow line. "Man trail!"

Zach contributed his left hand to the challenge of steering, and they both charted the course from the ground up. By the time they reached the Double D, Ann's shoulders were tied up in knots, and she said as much as she handed him the keys. The pickup's headlights flashed at their backs as Zach tucked her under his arm. "Zelda says you're designated for life."

"I may never drive again."

At the top of the porch steps they stomped snow off their boots, and he turned to her, shed a glove and brushed snow off her cheeks and hair. "I thought we made a good team."

"I guess we did. We're—"

His kiss was unexpectedly warm, decidedly appreciative. "You're a helluva woman, Ann. I've never met anyone…" He closed his eyes, touched his forehead to hers. "Except you," he whispered as his touch warmed to hers and hers to his. "But I didn't know it then. We were a lot younger, and I was a lot stupider."

"You weren't the same man, and I wasn't the same woman. Let's just leave it at that." She kissed him softly. "Thank you for another exciting evening."

Chapter Eight

Upstairs in her private bathroom, Ann chilled out in chin-to-toes heat. Steam in, madness out. Ah, yes, it was working for her. There was nothing like hot water for calming winter driving jitters and soothing the romantic soul.

She made herself get out while the room was still warm, before the water turned tepid and her hands and feet shriveled like colorless fruit. Feeling lush and languid, she dried her hair, brushed her teeth, slipped into a soft white nightgown that covered her body and looked pretty in the mirror. A plain woman in a pretty nightgown. Plain was just fine. Plain meant that nothing was sticking out too much. She was who she was, dance-floor flattery notwithstanding, and she'd had enough excitement for one evening.

But she was ready, just in case.

She turned the light off before she opened the bathroom door, relishing every last bit of juice left in the air. One small, old-fashioned wall sconce burned like a candle in the bedroom. Not that she couldn't find her bed in pitch dark, but a night-light felt welcoming.

Had she left the bedroom door open? *Tsk, tsk.* Just the kind of oversight that might be seen as an invitation. A woman trail.

Zach stood in the shadows, his forearm braced high on the doorjamb, shirt unbuttoned, chest bare, looking for all her world like an ad for blue jeans, man scent and lifetime fitness rolled into one.

Thank God, she thought. She'd nearly outsmarted herself. If he hadn't come, she would never know whether he'd missed the signs or just ignored them.

Dear God, she thought. He'd found his way, and now she had to find hers, from too big for her britches to too smart for her britches to no britches.

No britches, no brain? Crossing the cold bedroom floor on bare feet, she keenly felt the lack thereof.

Oh, come on, silly Ann. Which? Where of?

She smiled. *Wherefore are thou, britches and brain?*

Clearly he had no idea why she was smiling, or he would have laughed himself sick. Or simply smiled back.

"Don't tell me you're still cold." She traced the path between his shirt buttons with a bold finger—a cheeky game of dot to dot. "I'll have to suggest buttoning up."

"I don't make excuses." He pushed away from the door frame. "So you don't have to suggest anything. You can tell me flat out." With one blunt fingertip he traced the ridge of her collarbone to the base of her throat and then south to the satin trim around her night-gown's scoop neck. "Don't?" Slowly, he spread his hand over the upper swell of her breast. "Or don't stop?"

She lifted her chin, and he lowered his, giving her plenty of time. More than she wanted. She slid her arms under his shirt, around his back, spread her hands over his warm, moist skin and felt the ready power beneath it. His kiss came questing. His lips parted hers, tongue tested, tasted, took refuge in her mouth and found a playmate. They played where she lived. She chased him out. He sucked her in. They pushed back gently on their wants while they played out their needs, all in a kiss.

She grabbed fistfuls of his shirt and stepped back, back, back toward the bed, his kiss eagerly tagging after hers. The back of her leg hit home. She sat and slid her hands over his flat belly looking for more buttons. She found one and flicked it open, but he stopped her from proceeding further—pressed her hands, warm to warm and flat to flat—and bid her wait. Wait.

He eased her back and kissed her down, making her tingle in surprising places with small whispers and tender touches, all from a kiss. He took his sweet time finding expectant places—breasts waiting on tenter-hooks, nipples yearning for attention—and when he gave, he took his sweet time. All with a kiss.

His tongue traveled over her, from breast to belly, and when her hands flailed about, feeling for some piece of him, he claimed them, pinned them to her thighs and bid her wait. Wait.

His mouth was masterful. Every part of it played a role in bringing her down, down, down to the place where her wildness quivered, waiting. His lips crept up, and she went still. His tongue swept down, and she went wild. Her body wept, and he drank its tears. In his sweet, sweet time he tucked her hand into the front of his jeans and whispered, "Now, Annie. Touch me now."

The feel of him shocked her well-pleasured senses. She helped him shed his jeans, sheathed him in her hand and called to him by name. He braced himself over her on one arm while the other went to his back pocket for a condom. "Don't stop," he pleaded. She looked up, caught him unawares and saw raw need. In his eyes a flash of fury turned soft, amused. "Don't let him get away."

"Where would he go?"

"Crazy." He handled the condom, while she took care to handle him, stroke him, grow him. "Take him, Annie," he whispered hotly. "Take him home."

She welcomed him with a joyous sound that came from deep in her throat, and she gasped when he filled every part of her. It was her turn to plead, "Let me ride." He gave a sharp laugh, rolled to his back and lifted her without losing her. No more waiting. No holding anything back. It was their sweet time, and they used it to crawl inside each other, mend the heart and mark the mind. And once inside, they drew each other out, slowly stretching one into an exquisite extension of the other, a joining so taut, so sparkling and splendid, that it made time irrelevant.

"Listen to that wind," he whispered to her when they were again two bodies. He had gotten up to turn out the light, disappeared into the bathroom and returned with a towel to chase wetness and a glass of water to slake their winter's night thirst. In all ways he was thoughtful, and she took his ways to heart as she lay in his arms. "We were out there in that wild wind, Annie. Now we're here in your bed. *Damn,* this feels good, being wrapped up in you."

"The sound of the wind makes this still, small space seem absolutely secure, like a cocoon for two." She snuggled against his smooth chest. "I think I'm the one wrapped up in you."

"I'm pretty sure it's all about the feel of the holder. You know, like, eye of the beholder?"

"I get it." She smiled in the dark. "I'm feelin' it. Safe and warm. Good for me, Zach." She kissed his powerful chest. "Thank you for tonight. All of it."

"Your pleasure sure sweetens mine."

"Does it really? I think I made some silly noises. I tried to hold back, but finally I just—" she pumped her fist "—blasted off."

"Aw, I *love* it. Makes me feel fearsome, like one of those big catapults you see in books."

"Books like…"

"Like the ones I read. Surprised?"

"Oooh, touchy. I'm just asking what kind you *like.*"

"I was thinkin' of one that showed how those things

were put together. I came across a whole series of how-it's-made books with all kinds of diagrams and descriptions. Man, I just ate those babies up. Probably meant for kids. Probably what I should've been doing as a kid—gettin' into more books and less trouble."

"Do you…buy a lot of books?"

"I discovered these great places called libraries." He chuckled. "I don't have any place to keep books."

"We have tons of books in the den. Other places, too, but my father's den is filled with delicious books like that. Help yourself. Do you need a knife and fork?"

"I like to pick them apart with my hands. Suck all the juice out of the pictures and chew real slow on the words. I'm not fast, but I'm thorough."

She sighed. "I could name a few other things you do that way."

"Go ahead."

"Okay. Well." She traced his lower lip with her forefinger. "For one thing, you make love that way."

He caught her finger in his mouth, sucked it and let it go like candy on a stick. "Mmm, *we* make love that way. That was both of us, baby. That was ours." He grabbed her hand before it got away, pressed a wet kiss into her palm and then blew on it softly. She caught her breath, and he said, "That was exceptional."

"Once in a lifetime?"

"I hope not." He drew a deep breath and released it slowly. "You know, Annie, I'm interested in ancient history as long as it isn't mine."

"But you just gave me a stir-up-the-past opening

with that *less trouble* remark. I was supposed to ask what kind of trouble? And you were going to tell me what a bad boy you've been."

"I was?"

"Of course you were. And I was going to be pitter-pattingly impressed."

"With my bad self?"

"Absolutely."

"How many times have you been down this road?"

"Well…" She stroked his chest. "Let's just say that I, too, have a library card."

He laughed. "You're beautiful. How can I impress you?" He stroked the curves of her back. "Hmm? You want history? I've got trophies. I've got scars."

"I want to know more about this one." Her hand swept over his hip, her fingertips tracing the raised welts left by stitches that had knit his skin together.

"Bad ride and worse judgment. Ended up having surgery twice because I tried to get away without having any. Bein' laid up is the worst thing that can happen to a rodeo cowboy."

"It's not a good thing for anyone."

"You'll do anything to get back on the road. Take a drink, a pill, a shot, tape yourself up and cancel that follow-up appointment. You can't sit out too many go-rounds." He caressed her arm, kissed her shoulder. It felt as though he were preparing her for something she didn't want to hear. But his quiet admission surprised her. "Sally said she was there when Red Bull wiped up the arena with me. I'm glad you weren't."

"Me, too." She gave herself pause. "How long can you keep doing this?"

"I try not to ask myself that. It's who I am. I don't know what else I'm good for." He rolled to his back. "I mean *really* good. When I'm on top of my game, Annie, I can ride any bull I draw, and I can do it like nobody else. Comin' off a ride like that, I'm invincible, you know? I'm whole. I'm Zach Beaudry, bigger than life."

Arm across his middle, she touched the scar on his hip again and imagined a bull's horn ripping him open. "Maybe you should ride something else."

"The money's in bulls. Saddle bronc is classic, but it's the bull riding people pay to see. It's like football or heavyweight boxing or—"

"Gladiators?"

"Ancient history," he tossed out lightly.

She caressed his hip. A wound this grave might have sent him to his grave. Surely he was haunted by what might have been. "This isn't ancient, but I'll bet it feels like it sometimes."

"You got that right." He turned to her, bracing up on his elbow. "So, where's this den with all the books?"

"It's downstairs, off the dining room."

"You've never showed me around the house. This is the first time I've been upstairs."

"You've had one foot out the door the whole time you've been here. Just passing through. Like the dining room and the den, upstairs would be a detour."

"If you say so." He rolled over and flipped the covers back.

"Where are you going?"

"Find myself a book."

"You found your way here. Isn't that enough exploring for tonight?" She reached for him. "Please stay."

"You left me the first time." He turned, half in and waiting, half out and going. He wanted more than a simple invitation. "Not that I blame you, the state I must've been in. I wouldn't wanna sleep with me, either."

But? What was he looking for?

"Ancient history," she said as she tugged on his arm. "Come on, baby, it's cold outside."

Laughing, he came back, bracing over her on strong, straight arms. "I wanna know."

"I left because it was a little cramped."

"Aw, jeez." He dropped his head between his shoulders. Then he threw it back and sought her eyes in the dark. "The backseat?"

"Front seat."

He dropped his face to her covered belly, groaning all the way as though he was on number ninety-nine of a set of a hundred push-ups.

She pushed the splayed fingers of one hand into his hair. "I wonder what doing it in the pickup would be like now that I'm smaller."

"Probably not much better." He turned his head, rested the side of his face against her like a child resting his head in her lap. "I've got too many parts that stiffen up quick. Back then it was just the one."

"Have we missed each other's prime?"

They laughed together as he slid back under the

covers and took her in his arms again. "Can I take this off you?" He rucked her nightgown up to her waist, and she sat up for her unveiling. He tossed it toward the ceiling, and it floated to the floor like a white parachute. Instinctively she sought shelter in his embrace, and he gave her refuge without question. His hands investigated what his eyes could not, and she was okay with that. His hands had already proven themselves.

"Thank you for coming…prepared," she said.

"Thanks for being prepared for me to come." His chuckle trailed off. "You mean the condom?"

"The condom. I wasn't prepared for you to come. I wanted you to, but I wasn't prepared." Deep breath. "And it wasn't the first time."

"Seriously? You mean, I didn't…"

"We didn't, no. You'd had a lot to drink, of course, but I was perfectly sober." She lifted her head. "Does that make me too stupid to live?"

"Only if it makes two of us. Myself, I'm not feelin' it."

"Well, I'm O for two, and you just redeemed yourself, so…"

"Took me how many years? And we ain't dead yet, so…" He tucked her hair behind her ear and tapped her temple. "You got your water under the bridge and your bad boy redeemed. Give it a rest."

She nodded. "Stay."

He settled himself in her bed, and she settled herself in his arms. "This is nice." He swept her hair aside with his chin and pressed his lips to her temple. "But if you wanna try parking again, I'm game."

She laid her hand over the scar on his hip, kissed his mouth and held him close while the wind sang them to sleep.

Dusk settled into the prairie sky like a purpling bruise. The cows had been fed, and the water in the tank was still open, much to Zach's delight. His solar contraption was being sorely tested, and it was chugging along, just like the Double D and its hands. Zach was inspired by the way Hoolie kept at it, like an old truck pushing uphill. He knew what he was doing and why, and he knew he couldn't make it all the way unless he kept moving. Zach followed the old man's lead. There was no getting ahead of winter, but with luck and foresight there was a good chance of keeping up. According to Hoolie, last night's whiteout had only been a prelude.

"I guess I won't be fixin' anybody else's fence for a while." Zach wouldn't have cared if he never saw another wire stretcher after all the fixing he'd done on the Double D today. Winter feeding had gone into full swing earlier than usual, and Hoolie—he'd said it many times in the last hours—had only been one man.

"You don't need to fix nothin' for that ol' rattle-snake," Hoolie assured him as they headed into the barn with Kevin in tow. "He's got no proof the horses did him any damage. None."

"I should have gone over there straightaway." Zach liked to think of himself as a man of his word, especially when he'd made a big production of giving it. "Chances are there would've been no droppings, no hair caught in the barbed wire, nothing to show they'd been over there. And with him not having horses, any leavings would likely be ours." *Ours?* Little proprietary there, Beaudry. "Double D's. When horses come over for supper, they're gonna drop some road apples in your pantry."

"Which he didn't mention."

"But I said I'd check it out, and I didn't. And now the scene of the crime is buried in snow."

"Far as snow goes, you ain't seen nothin' yet. You won't be leavin' us anytime soon, Mr. Beaudry."

"At least not until I can fix that fence."

"If you say so," Hoolie said. "I say there's another front moving in, and more power to those horses to get food where they can. You're damn tootin', they can take it from Tutan. They're survivors, them mustangs. Cows are a different story, but they're sittin' pretty good for now, thanks to you boys."

"Think they'll be calling off school tomorrow?" Kevin wanted to know as he hung a hay fork on its wall hook.

"By the time Hoolie's storm of the century is over, school might be lookin' pretty damn good to you, Kevin."

"Just like Texas is gonna be lookin' good to you?" Kevin asked as he knelt to reward Baby for a day of shepherding.

"It always did, but no place is perfect. If it ain't cold and dry, it's hot and wet." But right now it was the wind having its way. After a calm day, it was picking up again, rattling in the rafters. Zach tipped his head back.

"I hear you, South Dakota," he shouted. Then he laughed. "The wind is the killer, isn't it? No matter what else the sky throws at us. What do they call it in Lakota, Kev?"

"The wind? *Taté*."

"*Taté* has all the power." Zach pretended to take a seat, left hand between his thighs, right hand reaching for the rafters. "Makes you wanna climb on his back and let 'er rip."

"Is it true they tie a rope around a bull's privates to make him twist around like that?" Kevin asked.

"It's called a flank strap—it's padded, comes off easy. It's just a little irritant, not a tiedown," Zach said. "Bulls and horses are ticklish around the flanks. You want them to kick up. You don't want them to run and hurt themselves. And the bull rope up front, that's for tying the *cowboy* down."

"That's how you stay on?"

"No way. Once all hell breaks loose, it's all about balance. The bull rope is kinda like a fulcrum. You know, like on a seesaw. I want the pressure toward the top of my palm so I can curl my fingers over the wrap and get just the right angle for my hand. That's my anchor, but my wrist gives me some play." Zach snatched a stray piece of twine off the floor, turned his left hand palm up and demonstrated his grip. "And then you get snug up on that fulcrum." He backed his hand into his crotch. "We call it crackin' your seat."

"Where can a guy get a bull rope?" Kevin wanted to know.

"I make my own. Made some for other guys, too. You can pay a lot for a good bull rope."

"You sell them?"

Zach shook his head. "Guess I could. I've got friends who won't ride without one of my ropes." He raised his brow. "I'd make you one, but it might get me in trouble with the women in your life."

"They don't want you to crack your seat." Kevin smiled.

Zach lifted one shoulder. "They don't want you to crack your *head*. That's the first thing they think about. That's why mamas don't want their babies growin' up to be cowboys."

"That's not the first thing a guy thinks to protect."

"Well, that's the difference between us and them." Zach laid a hand on Kevin's shoulder and put on a super-sober face. "I'm glad we had this talk, son."

Zach was never so glad to see a job completed. The cold was bone deep. It would take some serious fire to chase it away, and shootin' the breeze over mere burning wood wasn't serious enough. He needed—and this was a kick in the head—some down-home coziness. He needed a kitchen. Better yet, he needed a lap robe over his knees and a cushy sofa in front of a real fireplace, which was where Ann found him.

"How did it go?" Bless her beautiful hands, they were always bringing him something hot to drink.

"It got done." He inhaled the sweet steam and sipped. Apple. No kick to it. So, she missed perfection, but only by a few drops. "Hoolie's hurtin' pretty bad. We stoked up the woodstove in the bunkhouse, and Kevin's out there playing cards with him."

"How did you escape?"

"Easy. I said I was needed up at the house." He raised his brow. "Am I?"

"You've made such a difference between those two. They're always…" She demonstrated a seesaw with her hands. "All they needed was middle ground."

"A fulcrum, huh?" He chuckled. "I've been called a lot of things, but never that."

"I was just about to make you guys some sandwiches," she said. "There's plenty of roast beef left from dinner. How does that sound?"

"I'd rather hear the sound of you sittin' down beside me." He patted the space that needed filling, and she sat close. She was a bone warmer, all right. One hundred proof perfection. He stretched his leg, flexing his knee a couple of times as he put his arm around her. "If this weather keeps up the way Hoolie's predicting, you and Kevin might be in for a long Christmas vacation."

"Bad weather is no vacation on a ranch. No matter what you do, it's hard on the animals."

"We'll manage." He wasn't sure what managing would entail, but it pleased him to make the claim. "You've got a good setup here."

"I worry about the horses. So many of them are way past their prime." She rubbed his bum knee. "Which happens to the best of us, of course."

"We get another break in the weather tomorrow, I'll go out and check on 'em for you."

She shrugged. "I know it's the natural order of things. That's what the sanctuary is all about. And Sally's right. We need more land."

"For the horses, or for Sally?"

"For all of us, I guess. We're committed." She rubbed some more. "To the horses and to each other. All the way around."

"You don't feel like you're trapped?"

"This is a good place. I don't want to be anywhere else. I'm home." She straightened, staring at him as though he'd said something stupid. "But it's more than that, and I have to be willing to do more. Sally hates it that she can't be working out there through snow, sleet, wind and heat. I'm just a fair-weather ranch hand." She sighed. "I'm so lazy."

"Honey, you're crazy." He turned to her, tapped his thumb to his chest. "You're lookin' at lazy."

"You've been working your ass off all day."

"Seriously?" He took her hand off his knee, drew it across his thighs, tucked it against his back pocket and held it there. They were nose to nose. "Was there more there last night?"

"Annie, whatever happened to that—" they looked up to find Sally standing behind the sofa, staring down at them "—sandwich?"

Zach flashed a smile. "We were just about to make it."

"I see that." Sally smiled back. "Never mind the left-

overs, Annie. I'll get myself a can of something later."
Backpedaling, she added, "Worms, maybe."

Zach didn't know what to do with himself. Tip-off
time for some basketball game on TV sent Hoolie and
Kevin directly back to the bunkhouse after supper, but
not Zach. He didn't want to miss helping with the
dishes. Couldn't leave the kitchen without sweeping
the floor. He liked watching the way she stood on tiptoe
so much he almost missed the chance to get a new bag
of Kitty Kibble down for her. Then he watched her feed
the cat. He liked watching her do anything. Either he
was going stir-crazy, or frost wasn't the only thing he'd
been bitten by lately.

He was tempted to follow her upstairs when he heard
the water running in the bathtub, but he resisted by
plugging himself into Sally's doorway on the ground
floor. Sally was relaxing in a recliner with her nose in
a book. Why hadn't he thought of that? Get lost in a
book. *Stop thinking so damn much.*

Sally looked up and smiled. "Sorry for the interruption."

"Yeah. No. Don't mind me."

"I meant me," she said with a laugh. "Interrupting
your move on Annie."

"We weren't doin' anything. Much."

"Not as much as you wanted to?" She nodded toward
the desk chair. "Take a load off, cowboy."

Ah, an invitation. Now all he needed was *make
yourself at home.* Words like those might help him

figure out what to do with himself. He needed to make himself *something*. A home? A cowboy? Something more than a sorry interruption.

He surprised Sally by recognizing some of the photographs on her wall. There were posed pictures of animals—mostly bulls, a few horses, a lone dog—and action shots taken at rodeos. They reminisced a bit before Zach got around to the topic that had been on his mind all along. Sally's sister.

"Did you and Ann hit a lot of rodeos together back when you were contracting stock?"

"Nope, not many. Annie was either in school or working or…" She glanced at the gallery on the wall. "She wasn't a fan, Zach. It's obviously nothing personal."

"There was one time," he said quietly. He leaned forward, braced his elbows on his knees, laced fingers together and stared at the floor. "She was a fan one time, and that time it got very personal."

It felt like a full minute before Sally spoke. "You mean…you?" He glanced up. She looked stunned. "That was *you?*"

"She told you?"

"She told me about a cowboy. She never said who he was. It was a long time ago, but that was Annie's…" Shock turned to awe. "I can't believe that was you."

"Why not?" *Lay it on me, Sally. I gotta know.*

She pursed her lips and gave her head a tight shake. "You've been here all this time, and she hasn't said one word."

"And I didn't recognize her. She had to show me a picture. Damn my eyes, Sally, I didn't remember." He shook his head, confounded by old mistakes and new feelings, not the least of which was the need to unload on Sally. Hell, she'd asked for it. "Hard to believe I was ever that drunk or quite that stupid," he offered, hoping he wasn't alone.

Sally leaned across the arm of her chair and pulled a photo album off a tall bookshelf. "Roll over."

She gave a come-on gesture as she pushed the recliner upright. Zach took a ride in the desk chair and looked over her shoulder.

She opened the album, turned a few pages and landed on the girl Zach had met years ago in a cowboy bar. She had short, dark hair, noticeable face paint, and a round face. "This is her college portrait," Sally said. "The look wasn't her. She was looking for a way to bust loose. It never worked for her." She flipped back a few pages to a girl with longer, lighter hair, no makeup, wire glasses and a round face. A little more like Ann. A lot more *of* Ann. "This is her senior portrait from high school. Serious geek. Straight A's, student council, church choir, never—I mean *never*—got into any trouble. Basically shy. This girl lives inside the woman you know."

"There's a kid in all of us."

"I remember you from back then, Zach. I noticed you when you were starting out, and it wasn't just because you were good." She raised her brow appreciatively. "The kid in you doesn't look much different from the man I'm looking at right now."

"I'd like to kick that kid's butt. I still don't remember much about her, tell you the truth. I don't party like I used to, and that kid inside me is one of the reasons."

"I can*not* believe that was you," she repeated quietly.

"Yeah. Amazing what a few years'll do."

He reached over and turned back to the dark-haired Ann who was beginning to come back to him. It hadn't been said in so many words, but he didn't doubt he'd popped her…taken her…

Damn! Wasn't there a nice way to put it?

Deflowered.

Taken her flower?

Take her flowers. You owe her fruit and flowers by the truckload, Beaudry.

He drew a deep breath. "She sure looks different now."

"Better?" Sally demanded. He looked up, tried to determine the right answer from her hard stare. "Sexier?" She wasn't giving him his full thirty seconds.

Place your bet, Beaudry.

"I ain't gonna lie. When I first saw her, I thought I'd arrived at the pearly gates. Kinda glad it was your front porch."

"But that wasn't *the first* time you saw her." She nodded toward the college picture. "She was twenty years old there."

"I don't remember much about *either* time we first met, so that tells you something. No, it tells *me* something." He banished the tell with a wave and a laugh. "Too stupid to live, too ornery to die. Hell, I knew there was something familiar about her, and it was driving me crazy, trying to figure it out. I mean, she's got me—"

"*She's* got *you?* Why are men such boneheads sometimes?"

"Because we can't keep it up 24-7." He touched the picture with gentle fingers. "I almost did the right thing. But a girl like that—sweet and shy—buying her a drink, chattin' her up and then walking away would have been…" he nodded, acknowledging "…the right thing."

"*She* could've walked away." She gave him a closer look. "Right? She was free to walk away."

"Yeah. Sure." He shrugged. "I wish I could remember every detail, but, hell, it was *one night.*"

"And not exactly one in a million."

"Critical time, though. I'd been with a woman for two years. More or less. We'd split up for what turned out to be the last time." Again he looked at the picture. "College girl. I remember she told me she was just finishing up. I remember seeing her come in the door and thinking this girl looked as lost as I felt."

"So you were doing her a favor?"

"I was goin' with the flow. She was gone the next day."

"You didn't look for her?"

"I think I asked around. Or maybe I looked around a little bit. Hell, I don't know. Maybe I looked the other way." He leaned back in his chair and looked at the ceiling. "That's probably what I did. And, yeah, I went on down the road. I'm a cowboy. That's what we do."

"And you do it very well. Personally, I like that. It's part of the image. But my sister—"

"Your sister doesn't do *image*." Appearing in the doorway, Ann startled them both. "A complete makeover, and still no image."

Zach hung his head.

Sally squirmed. "How long have you been—"

"Long enough. I've already showed him one, Sally. You don't have to…" Ann sauntered close to the two chairs and craned her neck for a look at the image on display. "Why do you keep all those old pictures?"

"They're precious to me, Annie."

"You have no right to show them around."

"Why not? This is a family album. See?" Sally showed her the words embossed on the brown leather cover. "You're my family. People show family pictures all the time. There's nothing wrong with these pictures. There was nothing wrong with you."

"That's easy for you to say. You're not me."

"No, I'm not. I'm me. Don't you have a few pictures of me? Before and after pictures?" Sally gave a tight smile. "Do you show them around, Annie?"

"Okay, this is my fault," Zach said. "I asked the wrong question. I don't remember exactly what it was, but the answer was a doozy."

"We've already established that your memory is in sad shape," Ann said.

"Guess my head ain't quite hard enough."

"Hoolie's looking for you," Ann told him.

"Saved by the Hoolihan," Sally said with a dry laugh.

"All I know is, this is history." He laid his fist on the photo album. "Hell, I'm goin' down the road, all right. I got a family that I don't bother to…" He tapped the album a couple of times, and then he stood. "But I carry a load of old newspapers around with me so I can feel like they're part of my life." He shrugged. "'Course, I don't show them around. Wouldn't be good for the image."

His boots made his parting statement.

"So that's your cherry-plucking cowboy," Sally said quietly.

Ann stared at her sister, trying to look disgusted rather than horrified.

"I said, *plucking*. I take it you didn't tell him everything."

"So you filled him in?"

"If you were standing there long enough, you would know." Sally did what Ann called the flying eyebrow. "Or if you knew me."

"I thought I did."

"I played it by ear, and from what I heard, he has yet to learn *the rest of the story*."

"You know what?" Ann glanced back at the doorway. Empty. *He wouldn't*. She approached Sally's chair, purposefully if not menacingly. "A lifetime ago I had sex with the man. Big deal. That's all he knows and probably more than he needs to know. Or cares to know."

"Okay. Hands off. See?" Sally flashed both palms in sign of surrender. "He really likes you, Annie, and he's an attractive man."

"What happened to 'hands off'?"

One palm. From surrender to *hold on*. "But he's not good enough."

"For what?"

"For you. His best days are behind him."

"That's just plain—"

"It's just plain true. He had his chance, Annie. He's not good enough." Sally lifted one shoulder. "He's a cowboy."

"You *love* cowboys."

"*Big deal,*" Sally echoed. "That's the easy part. They're easy to love. The hard part is letting them go."

"And you know this for a fact *because*…?"

"Because I listen to country music. I'm just saying…"

"Maybe his *worst* days are behind him," Ann fired back.

"I wouldn't count on it."

Chapter Nine

"I've decided to accept your invitation," Zach said, deadpan. "I'm staying for Christmas."

"Good plan," said Ann, equally expressionless.

They stood shoulder to shoulder—okay, ear to shoulder—staring through the kitchen window at the profuse snowfall.

"When's Christmas?"

"Day after tomorrow," she said.

"That's what I thought. I'm glad we've got snow. Makes everything all Christmassy." His tone was cheerless. "We're socked in, aren't we?"

"We sure are."

"How's our list coming, Annie?" said an upbeat voice at their backs. "Did you get the turkey?"

"Dinner's covered," Ann told her sister.

"That's the most important part. Remind me not to call you Anal Annie ever again."

"That's on one of my lists." Ann subtly drew her hand down Zach's shirtsleeve as she turned away from the window. "Embarrassing things to remind Sally not to say."

"Not even in cyberspace. I was going to use the initials AA so you wouldn't be mistaken for some porn site."

"Speaking of Internet, how's your part of the Christmas list coming?"

"Well, the good news is, I got fifty percent off plus free shipping. The bad news is, that deal wasn't available until yesterday." Sally helped herself to a cup of coffee. "Kind of a half-full, half-empty situation."

"What's the opposite of anal retentive?" Ann wondered idly.

"When I was in the army, we just used the initials SNAFU," Hoolie said. "I don't know if it works for you girls, but it sure as hell works for this weather. We won't see any mail before spring unless they drop it out of a helicopter."

"All right, so the fruitcakes we were planning to give you guys might be past their sell-by date." Sally frowned at Ann. "What are you smiling about?"

"All the I-told-you-so's your AA sister has in store for you," Ann said. "All the canning we did last summer? We'll be eating tomatoes until hell freezes over, you said. Those apples you told me to leave on the ground? Apple butter. And all that rhubarb we put up for strawberry-rhubarb pie? Okay, the birds got the strawberries again, but I'll figure something out for rhubarb." Arms folded, Ann took a stand at the counter, hip to hip with her sister. "Well?"

Sally held out her hand, palm up. "Pass the crow."

"Canned or frozen?" Ann smiled. "I hate to see good roadkill go to waste."

"I won't ask where the turkey came from," Zach said.

"Smart man."

"I'm still in charge of oyster stew for Christmas Eve, right?" Seated at the table, Hoolie sipped his coffee. "Home-grown oysters. We might be a land-locked state, but we ain't oyster-less."

"Canned or frozen?" Kevin echoed without looking up from his game of solitaire.

"Ancient chuck wagon secret." Hoolie loved his Rocky Mountain oysters—deep-fried calves' testicles—but everyone knew them to be a once-a-year treat for the non-squeamish palate. And winter was not the right time of year. "You two got some kind of Indian specialty you can contribute?"

"We'll come up with something for them, won't we, Kev?" Zach moved in behind Kevin's chair and played a card for him. "Hunt up some wild pizza."

"I'm pretty good at rounding up Spam. I use a net."

"It'll be just like the first Thanksgiving," Ann said. "Great big potluck."

"Where don't ask, don't tell is good for everybody," Sally chirped.

But there was no chirping back. The barometric pressure was off the charts, and most chirpers had flown south weeks ago.

For the first time in years, Zach wanted Christmas, and he wasn't going to let the weather short-circuit any part of the celebration. There was no shortage of trimmings, thanks to the women of the house, who weren't expecting much else. The smaller the expectation, Zach reasoned, the greater the surprise.

It wasn't easy getting Hoolie and Kevin out of the kitchen, over the snowdrifts and through the machine-shop door, but Zach was on a mission. He fired up the space heaters and called for a huddle.

"All right, boys, who's got presents for Ann and Sally?" Zach's gaze ping-ponged from face to face. "Nobody?"

"I'm like Sally." Hoolie wiped his nose on the back of his cowhide glove. "Didn't get my order in soon enough."

"I didn't even get my mother anything," Kevin said.

"I hear you, man. My mother should've disowned me a long time ago." Zach clapped his gloved hand on the boy's padded shoulder. "We're gonna do phone calls. Right? That's what they want most. That's what they say, anyway. Phone calls and grandchildren. We'll call."

"What are we gonna do about Sally and…Miss Drexler?"

"We're gonna make them something." Zach pulled his plan out of the back pocket of his jeans and spread it out on the tool bench. He'd thought about it, sketched it out, even pictured it full of flowers and fruit. "A critter-proof strawberry patch, kinda like my mother's.

My dad made it for her. If Hoolie's willing to part with some of that junk he's got piled up behind the machine shop…"

"That's not junk. That's salvage."

"That's what I meant. We're gonna recycle it."

"Miss Drexler'll love that," Kevin said. "She's always talking about creative recycling. She uses it as an excuse to make us write. One time she put out a box of stuff people throw away and told us to write about other ways to use it. Stuff like pop bottles, plastic jugs, even a lightbulb. Dude next to me says, 'Either she's cooler than we thought, or she doesn't get it.'" He glanced at Zach and shrugged. "She didn't get it."

"Didn't get what?" Hoolie demanded.

Zach filled him in. "Stuff they could use to make bongs."

"A bong is—"

"I know what a bong is," Hoolie said. "You think I was born yesterday?"

Zach chuckled. "Nobody's makin' that mistake." The opening was huge, and he figured better him than Kevin. As for who *they* might be, Zach would have to think about that one, maybe pick it up again down the road.

"What I wanna know is, who's *they?*"

Thanks, Hoolie. "Junkies."

"People who collect junk," Kevin said.

Zach smiled. "Which is not the same as salvage, Hoolie. Now here's what I'm thinking." He'd sketched out a tiered planter made from farm-implement parts.

He'd figured in hooks for adding netting when the birds started going after the fruit.

"Here's the way you keep the tunnel diggers out. I read about this—you bury chicken wire." He turned to page two. Doodles on sticks. "And here's the best part, these little junkyard people. Like scarecrows, only more original. They call it yard art. We make these today, wrap 'em up and put 'em under the tree." He glanced at Hoolie. "I don't know what we use for wrapping."

"Junkyard paper." Hoolie was getting into it.

"And cowboy ribbon." Kevin ran his finger down the page, from bug-eyed doodle head to stake-in-the-ground point. "How do we stick the junk together?"

"You know anything about welding?" Hoolie asked, and Kevin shook his head. "Well, I do. And you will."

"Cool."

Zach stamped the plan with the end of his fist. *Game on.* "I guess it'll be up to you two guys to set it all up next spring."

"Maybe."

"We gotta do it, Hoolie. Otherwise—"

"Maybe it'll be just the two of us. Maybe not." Hoolie zipped his parka to his chin. "You won't be leaving us today for sure, so let's get them cows fed before we start playin' artist. That's one hat I ain't tried on yet."

Zach snatched Hoolie's stocking cap off—"Hey!"— tucked the edge under, and laid it on the old man's ruffled white hair like a beret. "They wear it kinda cocked to one side," he said, making the adjustment. Hoolie posed with an imaginary brush, swished imaginary paint over Zach's smirk, and prompted real laughter.

Christmas Eve would be remembered by most South Dakotans as just one more day in The Worst Christmas Season Ever, but Ann would never see it that way. No matter what else followed, her little corner of the big white blanket would always have a silver lining in the shape of a cowboy's belt buckle. Not that Zach actually wore a trophy buckle, but she liked the image, and she planned to bank it in her memory.

Her three hardworking men were late for supper for the second night in a row, but they didn't seem concerned about their stomachs. Or the weather. Or the long hours they'd been putting in. They burst through the back door all cherry-faced and animated as though they'd just bested the neighbor's kids downhill, umpteen runs out of a whole bunch.

But supper would not be cold.

"We were beginning to worry about you guys," Ann said as she wrapped some crusty rolls in foil for an oven warming. "It's been dark for hours."

"Come darkening sky, come blowing snow, a cowboy's work is never…" Zach rubbed his hands together briskly as he looked to Kevin for help.

"Slow!"

Zach high-fived his fellow poet. Hoolie's laugh was a full register higher than normal. Ann exchanged what's-up glances with Sally, who was sitting at the table nursing a cup of chamomile tea. It was Christmas

Eve, and their kitchen had just been taken over by three overgrown boys acting as though they'd heard jingling in the air on their way in the house.

"You weren't out looking for those horses, were you?" Ann touched the side of the kettle on the stove. Still warm.

"Which horses?"

"Well, that bunch of older…" She turned from the stove and found three pairs of expectant eyes. "Never mind. They'll be fine. We couldn't figure out what could be keeping you from coming in for supper. *On Christmas Eve.*"

"Is it Christmas Eve already?" Zach tapped Kevin's chest with the back of his hand. "Did you hear that, boys? Tomorrow's Christmas."

Ann glanced at Sally. "I think they've been watching old movies."

"And swilling Christmas cheer."

"We've been preparing a surprise for our bosses," Zach protested with a proud grin. "Lost track of time."

"Haven't had anything to drink," Hoolie claimed.

"Or eat," said Kevin as he pulled a chair out from the table.

"What's the surprise?" Sally asked offhandedly between sips of tea.

"Well, we practiced some Christmas songs." Zach claimed the chair at the end of the table. "But we need a little something to eat first."

"And a whole lotta something to drink," Hoolie said.

"You're in luck." Ann took three soup bowls down from the cupboard. "We have a lotta cider."

After supper, Ann served hot cider and tree-shaped cookies in the living room. Tiny white lights twinkled amid live and fake boughs alike, and the aroma of apples and cinnamon mixed with the heady scent of pine. Nobody cared that the floor beneath the tree was bare or speculated whether the snow streaking horizontally past the windows came from the sky or the ground. Remarkably, Ann shared in the contentment. It was Christmas. They were five celebrating as one.

"This is good." Zach raised his clear glass mug of cider. "It tastes a little…"

"Hard," Sally announced with a smile. "Annie has her recipes, I have mine."

"What's hard?" Kevin drank from his holly emblazoned mug. "Tastes like hot apple juice."

"Yours is regular cider, and don't you forget it." Ann would not be accused of serving alcohol of any kind to her students.

Kevin tried for a peek into Hoolie's cup. "Is yours different? Can I taste it?"

Hoolie drew his drink in close to the chest. "You've got a good singin' voice, boy. Mine needs lubricant."

"Whenever you're ready," Ann said. "I'm sorry we don't have a piano."

"How 'bout a keyboard?" Zach asked, and she shook her head with a smile. "Change of plans, boys. We can't do 'Jingle Bells' without a piano."

"Yeah, we can." Kevin sprang from the sofa and plucked three tinkling ornaments from the tree. He gave them a shake. "We have bells."

"Come on, Hoolie." Zach's knee gave a crack as he rose from his chair. He pulled Hoolie up by the arm, and they both laughed at his joints' multiple rejoinder. "The Disjointed Double D Trio."

The trio performed again after another round of cider, and they were adorable. Ann doubted that practicing Christmas carols was what had made them late for supper, but the fun they were having was infectious. She couldn't think of a better gift.

It was long past midnight when Zach started sneaking around with another trek through the snow. Back in the mudroom he removed snow-covered clothes— all but his precious hat—without making much noise, shouldered three bulky packages and made his way in the dark past table lamps and glass doodads without slipping around in his socks or bashing his shins. Hoolie and Kevin had wrapped their creations with feed sacks and twine. They were pretty proud of the way they'd cut off the ingredients lists, put the horse pictures front and center, and tied in a few sprigs of pine. They'd each made a sculpture on a stake, but they'd agreed they'd all sign the three packages. Kneeling in the dark beside the Christmas tree, Zach was deep into putting his signature on the third pack when he got caught.

"Santa?"

Zach transferred his smile from his name to Ann's sweet face. "Just one of his hands. Santa blew in, dropped these off and blew away again. Amazing." He slid the package under the tree, stood, tucked his thumbs into the front pockets of his jeans and eyed her armful of pretty packages. "What've you got here?"

"He dropped these off, too." The bottom of her long white robe puddled around her as she knelt to arrange her packages among his.

"Come darkening sky, come blowing snow." He offered her a hand.

"Santa's a cowboy?"

"He's anything you want him to be." He drew her up and into his arms. "Make a wish. It's the wishing hour."

"How does one wish on a cowboy?"

"Easy." He smiled as he slid his hands over her bottom and pressed her against him. "You rub his wishbone."

Her arms snaked around his back, and she smiled up at him. "No matter what the wish?"

"You got it, baby." He was thinking *angel,* the way she looked in the soft glow of the tree lights. "All wishes granted in the wishing hour."

"What if it's a really big one?"

He grinned. "All yours."

"What if wishes were horses?"

"Mmm, I'd beg you to ride."

"Oh, dear." She tucked her face under his chin and breathed against his neck. She was killing him softly, and he was loving it. What a gift. "You've always been a looker, but now you talk pretty, too. You're more dangerous now than you ever were, Zach Beaudry."

"What you see is what you get, honey. Merry Christmas." He leaned back—reluctantly, but he was missing something. "Wait a minute. What horses? You thought we went out after some horses." He cupped her soft face in his rough hand. "What's bothering you?"

"The older ones. But they'll be—"

"Fine. You said that." Hands on her shoulders, he moved her apart from him and gave her a hard look. "You don't believe it."

"Some of them won't make it, and that's natural. But I hear the wind, and I see those snowdrifts, and I imagine them…suffering. I know." Her hands slid away. "I know it's part of life."

"You want me to check on them?"

"In this weather? Absolutely not."

"What do you want me to do?"

"Just listen, I guess. Tell me there's nothing to worry about."

"I can't say that. I can tell you it's not gonna help." He pulled her into his arms again and whispered, "But I hear you."

"Oh, dear. Now you're a triple threat."

He chuckled as he rubbed her back. "I'm no threat. You don't wanna ride, we'll walk. Slow and easy."

"It's been good," she said with a sigh, "having you here. You've been good for all of us."

He leaned back, questioning her with a look. "You sound like you're handin' me my hat."

"Why would I do that?" She snatched the hat from his head, tucked it behind her back and gave a saucy smile. "When do you ever take it off ? Mealtime. Bedtime. Presumably bath time, although I would have—"

He made a quick grab for the hat, but her defensive jump was quicker.

"—no way of knowing for sure. There's no way I'm handing it to you. I've been plotting this for some time. You really won't go anywhere without this hat." She jerked back from another futile attempt to recover his property. "Will you?"

"Damn right I won't."

"Are you hungry?" she teased. He put his hands on her shoulders and shook his head. "Dirty?"

He lowered his head, eyes twinkling. "How do you mean?"

"You smell like lemon peel and cedar shavings in the snow, so that eliminates mealtime and bath time. That leaves …" He made a grab behind her back for the hat, but she dodged it. "Of the no-hat activities, that leaves—"

"I thought everyone was in bed," Sally again. Grinning and bearing gifts. "Don't mind me. I'm gonna sneak these under the tree." She sashayed around them, keeping her smug grin on. "I'm glad I got your scent right, Zach. Lemon peel." She sniffed the first package, put it under the tree, sniffed another package, flashed a smile. "Cedar shavings."

The world was white and sunny on Christmas morning. Ann watched Kevin and Hoolie make their way toward the back door, slogging through snowdrifts and squinting against otherworldly brightness as she cheered them on.

"Come on, you two, it's Christmas! We've got sugar-plums to eat and presents to open."

Hoolie shaded squinty eyes with a leathery hand. "Keep talkin', little sister. I'm following your voice."

"Where are your gloves, Hoolie?"

"Not *that* voice. Your respectin'-your-elders voice."

"I got snow in my boot," Kevin complained.

"Okay, follow this." She swung the door back and forth as she called out like a street vendor. "French toast. Real maple syrup from Minnesota. Fresh from the fridge Florida orange juice. Hot Colombian coffee."

"Annie, you're letting the cold in," Sally shouted from the kitchen.

Ann was ready with a broom for sweeping the snow off their jeans. "Take off your boots and put these on." She traded the broom for two pairs of moccasin-shaped slippers. "I made them from old wool sweaters. I felted the wool."

"*Felted,* Miss Drexler?" Kevin examined the brown footwear, tried one on, looked up and grinned. "It's *felt,* isn't it? You been out of school too long."

"Felting is a process whereby you boil something knitted from wool yarn, and then you…" Smiled when she realized she'd slipped into her teacher's voice. "Apparently not long enough."

"No, tell me." He hung his wet socks on a hook. "I must be learning something, huh? Feel, felt… felted?"

"Not the same, but good try." She stopped short of putting her arm around the boy's shoulders and giving a squeeze. For better or worse, a teacher was never really out of school. "We'll conjugate over breakfast."

But a woman was never without her inner little girl, who would not be denied on Christmas. One minute the woman was pushing French toast—"I made enough for a whole posse"—and the next the little girl was squirming in her chair. "Hurry up, you guys. I can't wait to see what's in those big, long packages."

"She's always been like this at Christmas." Hoolie grinned at each of his cohorts in turn before confessing, "Truth is, I can't wait to see you open those packages."

Ann couldn't remember a better Christmas morning. She'd always enjoyed the preparation, the anticipation, the sounds and flavors and colors of the season. It was the only time she trusted surprises. As a child she'd been told that holiday surprises came from angels, and she'd always wanted to see them. When she and Sally opened the three long, skinny packages, she knew she was looking at them. Her three angels. They could barely contain their pleasure in seeing their sculptures in her and Sally's hands.

The figures, they said, represented the three of them. They'd used nuts and bolts, horseshoes and tack fastenings, bits of tools and machinery that only the artist could identify. And they were, according to Zach, "Works of art, straight from the heart." Kevin had made Zach, complete with a cocky cowboy hat, carrying a bull rope with a little bell. Zach had given Hoolie a horse, and Hoolie had fashioned a dog for Kevin. If three charming "scarecrows" were not enough, the pledge to build a strawberry planter like the one in Zach's drawing nearly brought Ann to tears, especially when he told her it would be "just like the one my dad made for my mom."

"And speaking of your mom," she reminded quietly.

"I'll call," he promised. "When we're between go-rounds here. I don't wanna miss anything."

"It's your turn." She started pulling more packages out from under the tree, reading names and handing them to Kevin. "The youngest gets to deliver," she explained. "So, tag! You're it."

In addition to the slippers, Ann had knit four scarves, and Sally had made hatbands and scented soap.

"You know what?" Kevin said as he sat back on his slippered heels and surveyed the scraps of colored paper and bits of ribbon and twine. "This is cool. This is the way all my grandmas do. They make stuff for gifts. All the time. Quilts, clothes, earrings, hatbands, all hand-made." He turned the glow of his novel-idea bulb on Zach. "So who needs stores?"

"Careful, Kev." Zach play-punched the boy's shoulder. "You're talkin' to the son of a storekeeper."

"Oh, yeah. 'Course, we gotta have food."

"Speaking of which…" Ann glanced at her mother's mantel clock. "I'd better get that turkey in the oven. I'm already behind schedule."

"Miss Drexler's back," Kevin announced.

"Just in time," Sally said. "I can do the mashed potatoes, but the fancy turkey is too complicated for this cowgirl."

"How about the Funky Chicken?" Ann quipped. She

was rewarded with a chorus of groans. "Come on, you guys, that was funny."

They laughed all the way to the kitchen, where one more cup of coffee went along with cleaning up from one meal and starting the next. Everyone cheerfully pitched in. Ann hauled out a bag of red potatoes, called her sister's name and tossed her a potato as soon as she turned.

Sally made the catch.

"Show us how to do the Mashed Potato," Ann said.

"How old do you think I *am?*" She grinned and flapped her arms, bent at the elbow. "Here's the Funky Chicken." The potato flew back to Ann. "Your turn, Annie. They sang. I danced. Which of your talents will you be entertaining us with?"

"My French horn is packed away with my tutu. I think I can still recite the prologue to the *Canterbury Tales*."

"I'm on vacation," Kevin said.

"I'm not. I've got stock to feed." Hoolie paused on his way to the mudroom. "You wanna push some snow around, Kevin?"

When the equipment was motorized, Hoolie didn't have to ask twice.

"And I helped you memorize that thing way back when, which earned me a Get Out Of Jail Free card." Sally glanced at the clock. "I need a quick nap, and then I'll get after those potatoes."

"What about you?" Ann asked Zach, who'd been drying dishes. Out of the corner of her eye she caught Sally's bye-bye wave.

Zach flipped the dish towel over his shoulder and

nodded toward the counter and the assembly of ingredients for the meal Ann was about to prepare. "I'd listen to you recite from the labels on all those cans if it would help get that turkey cookin'."

"It's going to be a little later than I planned, but…" She took a plastic bag from the refrigerator and held it up proudly. "I do have the stuffing all made."

"Let me poke it into the bird." He slipped his arm around her waist.

But not without a woman's help, as it turned out—help Ann was happy to provide. He was like a kid discovering worms in mud. He couldn't resist playing with the "bag of guts," but the stuffing was not as much fun to handle. "It feels like it's already been eaten."

She gave him a spoon. "Did you find the neck?"

Up to his elbows in raw turkey, he leaned over and nuzzled hers.

She shivered as a pleasured sound escaped her throat, but her eyes were focused on his hands. "Go deeper," she said, and he flicked his tongue at the base of her earlobe. She squealed. "It has to be in there!"

He came away laughing. "Be patient, woman. Let me finish this first. Hey, look, the poker's packed inside." He dangled the turkey neck between their noses.

"Stuff it, cowboy."

Suddenly he was motivated, and soon dinner was in the oven.

Ann couldn't stand to stay inside when Zach went out to help "the boys." The air was cold and crisp, and the sunlight eased the labor and bolstered the good cheer. Zach boasted of his phone call, but Kevin had one-upped him by calling his mother as soon as he woke up. Zach came back at the boy with a snowball, and a two-on-two exchange ensued. Ann took Kevin's side. They declared victory when Hoolie cussed first. He'd gotten snow down his neck.

Daylight was drawing down when they went inside looking for warmth, but the house was murky and cool. Ann peered into the kitchen and found her sister sitting at the table and wrapped in a blanket.

"Sally, why are you sitting here in the dark?"

"I just woke up." Sally adjusted the blanket around her shoulders as she stood. "The electricity went off. Almost two hours ago, from the looks of it." She nodded at the clock on the stove.

Ann dropped her second boot and darted for the oven. "The turkey!"

"Yeah, it's probably a lost cause," Sally said sadly. "The thermometer isn't even up to *stopped twitching*. Guess I won't be doing the mashed potatoes."

But Christmas dinner would not be lost. Strategically placed candles brightened the living room, where the fireplace took center stage. The meal began with a scavenger hunt and culminated with ugly food on pretty plates shared in good company. There were no complaints.

"Christmas potluck at its best," Ann said. "Hoolie, the Spam is sublime."

"I got more over in the bunkhouse. That and the

pickled eggs. I offered to share with you girls before, but you always turned your pretty little noses up."

Kevin was stretched out on the floor beside the dog. "Baby sure enjoyed that half-cooked turkey meat."

Baby was also enjoying holiday power-outage privileges in the house.

"This is good pie," Sally allowed, even though it was rhubarb. "Good thing we made some pies yesterday." Yesterday she'd wanted to skip the rhubarb and just do apple and cherry.

"All kinds of technology, and still we're at the mercy of the weather," Hoolie said.

"Not if we use our own brains as backup," Zach countered.

"I guess I'd rather have the technology as backup for my brain," Kevin said around a mouthful of cherry pie. He swallowed hard and waved his fork at his new mentors. "I like Zach's so-called cowboy ingenuity, and Hoolie's hundred years' experience is growing on me."

Zach winked at Ann. "The judge is gonna be lining 'em up at the Double D gate, Miss Drexler."

"Hey, when the goin' gets tough, the tough get smart."

"That little water heater you rigged up on the hearth is a good example of that, Kevin." Ann nodded toward the copper contraption suspended on a tripod over banked embers. "I'm going to use it as a humidifier even after the electricity comes back on. But for now…" She started gathering dishes.

"Sit," Sally ordered. "I'll take care of cleanup, but not until I'm good and ready."

"First baking and now dishes?" Ann stared in mock disbelief. "Where's my sister?"

Sally laughed. "Christmas is supposed to be full of surprises."

"This one sure makes the grade," Zach said.

They played cards and checkers and name that Christmas tune, made popcorn over the fire and told family stories. Different times, different families, not-so-different stories. There were tricks played and jokes made, lost bets and found pets, favorite foods and games, aunts and uncles. Good times and good people always kept the cup half-full.

Kevin fell asleep on the floor. Zach added wood to the fire. There were two sofas, and Hoolie was about to vacate his end of the one he was sharing with Ann.

"Stay where you are," Ann said as she tossed a throw around her shoulders.

"I'll be fine on the floor."

"Absolutely not," Ann insisted sleepily. "Age before beauty. That goes for you, too, Sally. You stay right where you are."

"You hear me offering up my position? I like being the elder sister, and this is my favorite sofa. As for beauty, well, I can always turn to the mirror and behold."

"We'll need more pillows and blankets." Ann stood. "Will you give me a hand, Zach?"

"Sure." Zach jabbed at the added logs, and the flames leaped to embrace them. Sparks danced in celebration.

"Yeah, I could use another pillow," Hoolie called

after Ann as Zach joined her in the shadows. "I gotta keep my knees—"

"They're not coming back," Sally informed Hoolie at the top of her whisper range. She tossed him one of her pillows. "Merry Christmas."

Chapter Ten

Ann paused in front of her door. Zach closed in behind her, cupped his hands around her upper arms, drew her back against him and encircled her shoulders with his arms. "I ain't sleepin' on the floor." He kissed the side of her neck and whispered, "Let's make our own fire."

She closed her eyes and tipped her head back. "Did you bring wood?"

"Oh, yeah." He gave a husky chuckle. "The kind that burns long and slow."

She turned in his arms. "I have kindling."

"Show me."

She pushed the throw off her shoulders and laid hands on the bottom of her sweater. He stopped her.

"Not here. We'll set the whole place aflame," he said as he led her by the hand, bypassing the bed.

"What are you d—"

"I haven't had a chance to clean up."

"It's too cold!"

"How do you want me? Ripe or—ow! What the hell?" He'd run into the vanity stool in the bathroom, where darkness reigned. "Or rank?"

She felt along his arm to see what part of his body he was nursing. "I don't want you injured."

"Too late." He was rubbing his foot. "Should've been wearing my new slippers. I'm bettin' there's still hot water in the tank."

"Betting what?" She seated herself on the side of the tub and turned the knob in question.

"One big toe and two big O's."

"Bet your own stuff, cowboy. Those O's are mine."

Her grin was lost in the dark, but his laugh wasn't. Running water—freezing to cold to cool—couldn't dampen that rich, warm sound. *Please be hot for him. Give him everything he wants, starting with...*

Yes! "You win. It's getting warm." She flipped the stopper lever.

He unzipped the starter lever and shucked his jeans. "After you."

"Uh-uh. This one's for you."

"What I mean is..." She heard his shirt slide over his head. "I win only *after* you win. How's the water?"

"Pretty..."

His hand met hers under the warm running water. His

arm met her nose, which she used to trace a path up to his shoulder and down, bumping over his collarbone and onto his mighty chest. He took her wet hand to his belly. The head of his penis skated across her wrist as she drew wide circles around his navel with the light touch of all four fingertips. He stood for her in every sense of the phrase until the catch in his breath declared his limit reached. He took her hand from him and drew her to her feet, lifting both arms over her head for a quick upper-body peel.

Her arms came down, crossed over each other and around her slim torso as she swayed toward him, inviting his warm embrace. But he caught her by the shoulders as he seated himself on the side of the tub and tended to her snap. And her zipper. And her hips, thighs, the backs of her knees, foot, foot—all set free. She heard her clothes swish across the floor, his hand slosh in the tub, and then he took his turn brushing wet fingertips across her belly.

"This one's for us," he whispered.

"But it's—"

He cut her off with kisses—belly, breast, neck, mouth—and mouth to mouth he drew her into the tub with him, positioned her legs around him so that their extremities touched but not their centers. The water was warm. The air was cold. The soap was silky, and the hands were slow, searching, sensitive to every discovery.

It was only a prelude. Before inner quivers became outer shivers they dried each other off, dove under her down comforter and commenced a rubbing, hugging, kissing frenzy, wildly funny at first—two winter skinny-dippers chasing each other's chilblains—and then purely wild. He touched her until she whispered *oh, oh, oh.* He nuzzled her until she nearly died, suckled her until she nearly cried, tongued her until she bit his hand. He was laughing when he slid inside her, and she rode his joy beyond walls and wind, well into the winter-night sky.

They dozed a little. Cuddled a lot. He was deliciously spent, but unwilling to take a chance on an Ann-less dream.

"Did you call home today?" she asked.

The warm breath of her words rolled across his chest, and his nipple puckered defiantly. "Home?"

"Your family." She pushed her small fist into his side. "Your *mother,* bad boy."

"When did I have…" He couldn't say it. *No time* was a lie he could tell himself, but not Ann. "I'll do it tomorrow for sure."

Her fist uncurled and became a soothing hand. "Why is it so hard?"

"It isn't hard. All I gotta do is pick up the phone. Dial the number." He drew a deep breath and let it slide quickly through his nose. "Get through the first question."

In a chipper voice she took up the role. "How are you, Zach?"

She sounded nothing like his mother, thank God. And he knew his lines. "I'm doin' great, Ma. I'm, uh… I'm here in…"

"Are you well?"

"Yeah." He smiled into the dark. "*Yeah*. Look, Ma, no cast. I don't hardly hurt at all."

"Are you safe and warm?"

"You wouldn't believe how warm." He pressed a kiss into Ann's hair and turned serious. "I don't know about safe. Is it safe to give my heart away?"

"That's a great line, Zach. Are you writing cowboy music these days?"

So much for serious. "Not yet. Gotta earn some real cowboy stripes first. I'm workin' on it." *Why wasn't it working?*

"So you're warm and well, and you're working. You're eating right and getting enough rest?"

"Yep."

"That's what I need to hear, Zach."

"Come on, Ma. You've got one more question."

"What are you doing right now?"

"You don't wanna know the details. What you wanna know is…" *Give it another shot, Beaudry. See what she says.* "Have you found someone, Zachary?"

The game was over. Ann let silence be the signal. A moment of silence for all the someones who had come before, herself included. He was too smooth by half, and she was not. She would joke with him about sex, but not love, if that was what he was hinting at.

"Zachary." Delayed echo. "Is it a family name?"

He was quiet for a moment. Then he shifted slightly, as though he were physically accepting the change of tone. Topic. Territory. Wherever they'd drifted.

"Kind of. The way they tell it, Ma named my brother,

and Dad got to pick a name for me. So…" He drew a deep breath. "In 1927, Babe Ruth hit his sixtieth home run of the season in a game with the Washington Senators. The pitcher was Zach Zachary. A great moment in baseball history, and my dad thought it was a cool name. He loved baseball. He knew all the stats. The Senators became the Minnesota Twins. I don't remember a whole lot about my dad, but Sam…"

"Your brother, Sam."

"Yeah, Sam, he picked up where my dad left off. I guess my dad used to call me Short Stuff, and Sam changed it to Shortstop. When kids started calling me Shorty, I asked Sam to cut it out, and he did. Put an end to Shorty, right then and there. That's my brother, Sam. He's the Man." He chuckled. "Guess it could've been worse. You could be sleepin' with Babe."

"I like Zachary. I like Zach. I'd name a…" She snapped the tail off that puppy in a hurry. "You know, Zach, they're not that far away."

"No, they're not. When I leave here…" He hooked his leg over both of hers. Not much hair on either side. "Maybe I'll head up that way for a couple days."

"On your way to Texas?"

"On my way to catch up with the rodeo circuit." He nuzzled her hair and gave her his lonesome cowboy mantra. "Goin' down the road."

"What are you looking for, Zach?"

"Now you really sound like Ma." He gave her what she took to be a sample of the real Ma Beaudry's tone. "'A road is a way to get from place to place, Zachary.

There's no other end to it. Just like there's no end to chasing your tail.'" He sighed. "That's why it's hard to call. I been doin' it long enough now to know it's true."

"And the truth hurts?"

"Startin' to."

"Maybe it's time to get off the road."

"I'm not finished. I haven't done what I set out to do."

"You've done very well. You've won countless go-rounds. You've—"

"I've got nothing to show for it." He gave a humorless chuckle. "I think that's the first time I've said that out loud."

"Zachary…" She took a deep breath. "Have you found someone?"

"I don't know. Have I? You tell me." He laughed. "Damn, you women don't leave a man a scrap of cover, do you?"

"Cover for what? Your pride?" She patted his chest. "You're safe, Zach. Let it go."

"I don't feel safe. I feel hot and cold, smart and stupid, high and low—hell, I've never felt this insecure. And I ride bulls for a living."

As dark as it was, she saw herself in his eyes. Who was she to ask him to step out in the open?

"I was all those things the night I met you, Zach." She felt his quick tension, and she cut him off before he could turn her away from the memory. "No, this isn't about guilt. I promise. I was overdue to hatch, and I went through that whole range of feelings while I summoned the strength to peck on my shell from the inside. But it was a hard shell. A very hard shell."

"You needed a strong pecker to go at it from the outside, and I was more than—"

She smacked him where she'd patted before. "What happened to the cowboy poet?"

"Like they say, he had you at hello. Back then if he scored on his bull, he scored with hello."

She braced up, making a little tent over him with the covers over her head. "I don't know whether to laugh or cry."

"Don't do either, honey. That was then. The truth didn't hurt because I believed my own bull."

"Well, it wasn't the truth that set me free." She struck the tent and settled back down. "It was that strong pecker."

"I was good for something, then."

"You changed my life."

Any questions?

No? Well… "I missed two periods before I bought a pregnancy-testing kit."

He went still. Absolutely froze.

It was something. She wasn't sure what, but she took it as a good sign. She could tell him now. It would be okay.

"Two kits, actually. And then I went to a new doctor, who did another test. If the results had come up on a slot machine, I would have hit the jackpot." He didn't make a sound. Didn't bite. Didn't fly. Didn't move. "But I had a miscarriage, so…"

"So…"

So? So? What do you mean, so?

"So, I lost the baby." Calm. Cool. Matter-of-fact. *Just the facts, Annie.*

"Damn," he whispered.

She had no idea what that meant, either. She wasn't about to ask.

"Why didn't you…" Finally he moved. He pulled her closer to him. There was no need to finish his question.

But she needed to try out an answer.

"Because I didn't really know you, Zach. I had no idea what you'd say or do. I knew I'd been *very* foolish, and it was my predicament, and it was so crazy I didn't want to think about it." Her throat burned. Her eyes stung, but she was not, *not* going to get all teary. She drew a slow, deep, nerve-steadying breath. "If it had turned out…differently…I probably would have gotten in touch with you. Down the road."

His heart pounded against her ear.

"I'm sorry."

"For what?" She swallowed hard. "I'm not being flippant. What part of it are you sorry about?"

"All of it." He stroked her arm. "I'm sorry for being careless. Sorry you got pregnant, and I wasn't there. Sorry for…the loss."

"I was scared about being pregnant, didn't quite *believe* it was true even though I knew it was true. Which probably doesn't make sense to you, but…"

"No, it…it makes perfect sense."

"But when it happened—all that blood and the pain—well, when it was over, I expected to feel nothing but relief. It wasn't like that."

"What was it like?" he asked gently.

"Like a dream died inside me." She hadn't thought that one out, and it sounded melodramatic, but she rushed on. "I mean, obviously, the time for my child hadn't come, but I want children. I've imagined… The thing is, I had a little face in mind, little hands and feet. I really wanted to call you right then, when I felt so…empty, I guess. I wanted to tell someone."

"You told Sally, didn't you?"

"I told her about you. I didn't tell her about the baby. Because it was a pregnancy, you know? It was a baby that might have been. I didn't want to tell her because I was never one to do stupid things, and that's how my sister knew me. That was my only… It was my big, my main…*thing*. I do *good*. I don't do stupid."

"You're sure about that." She could feel the curve of his smile against her forehead. "Honey, I'm afraid you just *did* stupid."

"*I'm* not. I know I did good."

"Gettin' there. Closer, anyway." His smile became a kiss, and he whispered, "I hope. Pretty sure I'm on the road."

"I'm pretty sure we all are. But eight years ago when we crossed paths, we were so different. When I realized that we shared this one thing, this incredible surprise, you were the only one I wanted to tell. And I knew that would be foolish. So I've kept it to myself, *never* said it out loud." She added quietly, "Until now."

Foolish. Foolish?

Zach couldn't say. He'd been pretty damn full of himself back then, but his mama hadn't raised no deadbeat. He could have made room for somebody else.

And then what? Would he have done right by them?

Thank God the road was long enough for a guy to make a few changes along the way.

"I'm glad you told me. I'm really sorry. I…" he took her hand from his chest and kissed her fingers "…don't know what else to say."

"You don't?" She shook her head. "I just handed you a mountain of trust, Zach. So now that I've given up my little scrap of cover and we're both naked in more ways than one, you don't know what to say?"

Yeah, he did. "I've found someone."

"No bull?"

"No way." He pressed her hand to his chest, as though his heartbeat somehow gave testimony. "It's the truth. I've found my someone."

Now what was he going to do about it?

He was gone the next morning. Possibly for good.

Ann woke to gray light, cold room, empty bed. If truth was beginning to bother him—and he'd said it was—then last night's big truth might have been this morning's big bother.

He could very well be on the road again. Possibly for his own good.

Possibly for hers.

She flipped the covers off, swung her legs over the side of the bed, sat up and thought about the possibilities.

But only for a couple of seconds. She was stark naked, and it was seriously cold.

Anyway, she wasn't feeling it. The cold, yes. Zach's absence, no. He was around here somewhere. He wouldn't leave her, not this way.

"He's out with Hoolie and Kevin." Sally handed Ann a steaming cup of coffee. "This is instant." Surprisingly, it came without loaded looks. "It's not great, but it works. They're doing chores. Hoolie's predicting more nasty weather, and nobody doubts him anymore."

"No electricity yet?" Rhetorical question, considering Sally was camped out next to the fireplace and making coffee from a makeshift kettle.

"Within the hour, they say. Did you miss it?"

Ann pressed her lips together, half coffee sip, half smile. "Not at all."

"What if he's not ready to settle down, Annie?"

Ann scowled. A loaded look for Sally's question. *Not welcome at the moment, big sister.*

"I don't want to see you get hurt," Sally said.

"Is that why you gave him the pictorial version of *Ann's Life So Far?*" They exchanged glances, apologies on both sides. Ann touched her sister's hand. "It's okay, Sally. I should be angry about it, and I'm not. And you know what? I'm pretty proud of myself for that."

"I'm proud of you for a whole lot more than that." Sally grabbed her hand and squeezed. "Zach cares about you. Anybody can see that. It's just that—"

"He's a cowboy. A *rodeo* cowboy, which means what? These days, bull riders can come from New York

City, where people's idea of a cowboy is a guy standing on the corner wearing hat, boots and whitey tighties. I mean, what's a *cowboy?*"

Ann had her sister laughing now, which was lovely, but not quite where she meant to go. So she shifted gears.

"Sally, the man's broken every bone in his body, just about. If he's got feet of clay besides, I've got no use for him." Ann knew doubt when she saw it, and she cut it off with a gesture. "No, I'm serious."

"Okay." Sally raised her brow. "Okay, now I'm worried about Zach. Wandering around on clay feet in his *tighty whities.*"

"Whatever, Sally. We had a little fun in the sack. Zach doesn't lack in the sack." She gave what was meant to be a cute smile. "If you need something to worry about, there're some horses out there that are probably too old and decrepit to survive in this kind of weather."

"Then some of them will die."

"That's right. Some of them will die. So worry about that, while I..." Ann cocked her head toward the kitchen. "Was that the back door?"

"I didn't hear anything. Go look."

She shook her head. Her throat prickled, and her face felt hot. Look out—tears coming on. And for no good reason. She'd been on top of the world a few minutes ago. Realistic, completely rational, ready for the next challenge. What was going on with her? Besides being in too deep with a man she hardly knew.

It happened all the time. Happened to a lot of women *all the time.* They got in, they got out. Inner conflict had to be part of the process, right? The ups were bound to be upper, the downs downer.

She'd blame PMS, but she wasn't much of a PMS-er.

"Cabin fever," she said, a little raspy.

"Are you kidding? This cabin's getting colder by the minute."

Ann shook her head again.

And then the lights came on. Not the one in her head, but the one *over*head. And on the Christmas tree, down the hall...

Ann gave an unconvincing little laugh. "I'll make sure everything's back on. You stay by the fire."

"I wasn't complaining, Annie. Take a breath." Sally grabbed her sister's arm to forestall her flight. "I thought you weren't mad about the pictures."

"I wasn't. I'm not. I shouldn't have brought it up. He didn't remember me. So what? I'm not the only one who's changed."

"Like you said, he's a rodeo cowboy. Not as good as he used to be, but—"

"He's not the man he used to be," Ann pointed out. "He's better."

"You would know," Sally said with a saucy glint in her eyes.

"Yes, I would." And sex, her tone attested, was only the beginning. "But I'm not sure he does."

Sally's sauce drained away. "Maybe you should tell him."

Hadn't she done that? *Doing good,* she'd said, and he'd said he was on the road.

Aren't we all.

So maybe she hadn't sounded all that sincere.

Ann shook her head. "It doesn't matter what I think. He has to be able to see it for himself."

"Sometimes it helps to see yourself in someone else's eyes. If this is one of those times, and if you're that someone, it damn well *does* matter what you think."

"What happened to—" A noise shot through her. "Definitely the back door."

She met Hoolie in the kitchen. "We're just coming in to warm up," he said, but Ann was fixated on the clatter in the mudroom.

Kevin appeared in the doorway. "That wind's pickin' up again."

"Spent the last hour clearing the way to the feed bunks, and they'll probably be drifted in again by nightfall."

"We'll just have to do it all over again tomorrow, huh? I'm really gettin' the hang of working that blade."

Words, words, words. Ann listened for more clatter, leaned for a glimpse of one more man.

"Where's Zach?" *And don't tell me...*

"He went out to check on some horses." Hoolie was poking around in the cupboards. "I see the power's back on. No coffee yet?"

"*Drove* out?"

Hoolie gave her a quizzical look, as though she'd used a four-letter word. Or a four-syllable one. "He went on horseback. Can't get out there in a pickup now, little sister. After this blows over, I might take another look at one o' them snowmobiles. Even if they do make more racket than a damn rock crusher."

"He's crazy." Ann looked to Kevin for some sign of concern, but he was headed for the refrigerator. "Hoolie, he'll freeze."

"He thinks he knows where they are. If he's right, it ain't that far."

"He said an hour, tops," Kevin supplied, even as he supplied himself with milk and orange juice.

Hadn't they just said the wind was picking up?

"How long has it been?" Ann asked.

"I don't know." Kevin was looking for cereal. "Feels like an hour."

"Hoolie?"

"Feels like an hour. Probably more like half."

"I'll go lookin' for him if you want me to," Kevin offered.

"Absolutely not." Ann reached over the boy's head and opened the cupboard that held the cereal. "This is my fault."

"What's your fault?" Hoolie demanded. "The man's been gone less than an hour, and he knows what he's doing. There's no fault to be had."

But there was. She'd as much as instructed him to round up those horses. Impossible for one man in this weather. Who did she think she was? Some Greek god sending a mortal man off to do or die?

Settle down, she told herself as she snatched a blanket off the back of a kitchen chair and started for the mudroom. Drama wasn't part of her nature.

Hoolie's familiar hand came from behind and landed on her shoulder.

"What are you gonna do?"

She turned and looked into his calm, caring, aging blue eyes. Shook her head. Didn't know. Had no idea.

He gave her shoulder a little squeeze. "We need you here. It ain't time to start worryin', but if that time comes, you're the best worrier we got."

"Yeah, Miss Drexler. We need you to be a worri*er,* not a worry-*ee.*" Kevin appeared at Hoolie's side. He smiled, sympathetic beyond his years. "Have I got those endings right?"

"Feels like they're right." She glanced toward the window. "Where does he think they are?"

"Ain't tellin'." Hoolie slipped his arm around her shoulders. "But if worryin' time comes, I know where to go look for him."

Ann busied herself with making everyone a hot meal and getting everyone to the table. *Everyone* was supposed to include Zach. He belonged in the empty chair. Well, one of two empty chairs—Ann wasn't sitting in hers, either.

"You're hovering," Sally informed her without looking up from her pancakes.

Darned mind reader.

Ann folded her arms and pushed out a sigh. "Should we call the sheriff?"

"He hasn't been gone that long," Hoolie said for the third or fifth time.

"If we wait too long, it'll be dark. And the wind…"

Sounded a lot worse than *picking up*. More like the prairie version of gale force. "I'm going to call the Tutans. They have snowmobiles."

"You're *not* calling the *Tutans*," Sally said.

Hoolie looked up from his breakfast. "Zach hasn't had time to get the job done yet. You gotta at least give him that. He, uh…" He cleared his throat, rubbed his clean-shaven chin on the back of his hand. "He said he needed to do this for you."

"But he doesn't. *He doesn't.*"

She marched into the mudroom and started bundling up. It didn't make much sense, but she couldn't stay inside. She had to feel the cold cut of the wind and see the top of the hill. If he didn't come riding over that hill soon, she'd call out…send out…go charging out…

She'd do *something*.

For the moment, she went charging back into the kitchen for a blanket. She found two.

Hoolie rose from his chair and blocked her second exit, arms akimbo. "Where do you think you're going, little sister?"

"Outside," she barked, and then she looked up at the man who'd become part of her landscape. He had eyes like her father's. The color was different. So was the shape. But it was a fatherly look, and it deserved a daughterly smile. "Out-siiide," she amended, imitating the rodeo cowboy's open-the-gate signal.

"That's my job," he said.

"I promise not to go any farther than the top of the corral fence. I'm going out to watch for him." She reassured the dear man with a hand on his cheek. "That's my job."

Draped in one blanket and seated on another, Ann hadn't been perched atop the corral fence long before a lone rider appeared, his horse trotting over the hill behind the homeplace. *Thank God.* He wasn't pushing any horses, but in this weather…

Wait a minute. A horse topped the rise behind him. And then another. Two more, and then another. They were following, noses to the ground, pausing momentarily and then moving along. Zach appeared to be dropping a trail. Of feed! The big bay and its rider moved at a measured pace, both meeting the wind head down, trusting each other, clearly following their instincts rather than their eyes.

Ann's heart soared. This was her reason for standing lookout—the sight of this man in this moment. Through wind and snow, hurt and health, thick and thin, he gave his best effort. The results hadn't always been this pretty, but he was no quitter.

Zach Beaudry was a cowboy.

The closer he got, the more there was to admire. In this weather a wild horse chase would have been futile. Zach was playing Pied Piper. Riding bareback, he'd slung feed bags over the horse's rump, and he was spreading oats instead of notes. He looked up, waved, led the horses to water and came to her to drink.

"You're a sight for sore eyes, all wrapped up in your blanket," he said as he dismounted.

She started down, he reached up, and they met on

the ground, face-to-face and smile to smile. "I have one for you," she said of the blanket she'd left flapping in the wind.

"I'll take half of yours." He took a two-handed hold on the blanket beneath her chin and lowered his head for the kiss she'd had waiting for him. They both stopped shivering. He smiled against her mouth, gave a deep chuckle and then a quick, exuberant kiss. He took her blanket, threw it over his shoulders and pulled her close under the wings he'd just made. "The Indian way, the man's the one who brings the courtin' robe, but I guess times have changed."

"Aren't you supposed to hold it over our heads in case we're being watched?"

"Let 'em watch." He kissed her again and then laid his cheek against hers. Smooth, hard, cold, welcome. "You're crazy, woman."

"Look who's talking." She moved her chin up and down for the feel of his face rubbing hers. "I promised Hoolie I wouldn't go out looking for you. Five more minutes and I would've broken that promise." She turned her head, brushed noses, grinned… "Cold nose." And turned the other cheek for a greeting on that side. "I see you rode bareback. Very smart."

"It was the only way I could get the horse to go out with me." He leaned back, gave grin for grin. "Cold nose, hot ass."

"The horse is a boy."

"When it's this cold, you don't look a warm body in the…whatever."

She laughed. "Your nose is cute when it's cold. Like Rudolph. Let's get your hot ass inside before it cools off."

"Gotta rub this boy down first." He clucked to the patient bay. The horse chomped on the bit and nodded vigorously. "Yeah, big guy, you earned it. Gotta throw these old hay burners some fuel, too."

They took care of the horses together.

"Look at our solar system, Annie," he said as they emerged hand in hand from the barn. She looked up. He gave her a shoulder bump. "I mean, our solar water heater." He pulled her to the edge of the tank the horses had drunk from earlier. Big chunks of ice floated on the surface. "It's still open, even with the electricity off for, what? Fifteen, sixteen hours? It was sunny yesterday. It *works*." He nodded, still staring at his handiwork. "Like me."

"Not like you." She squeezed his hand. "You're not passive. You're very—"

"You're the sun, Annie." He squeezed back. "I'm just baskin' in the sun."

"I love you."

He was quiet for a moment. Then he said quietly, "For what?"

"I didn't say, *thank you*." She looked him in the eye, demanded his full attention. "I said *I love you*."

"And I said, *for what?* For a red nose and a hot ass? What about all the beat-up parts?"

"I love you."

"Been kicked in the head a few times, but a guy would have to be brain-dead not to recognize—"

"I love you." She reached for the back of his neck

with her free hand and pulled his head down for another quick, hard kiss. "For *you*."

She had another kiss coming. His was slower, surer, less for making a point and more for giving a promise.

"I've got a strong heart, Annie, and it's all yours."

"I'll take it. We'll pin it to your sleeve with my name on it." Her hand slid from his neck to his cheek. "But the important question is, do you have any skin in the game?"

"Oh, yeah." He turned his lips to her palm. "And there's plenty more where that came from."

Chapter Eleven

Zach had a lot to feel good about that night, and it was time to add one more thing. A belated wish.

It came out smooth and strong despite the prickly lump in his throat. "Merry Christmas, Ma."

He looked up at Ann, smiled and nodded. "Yeah, I'm doin' good. No, really, I haven't broken anything lately." Ann smiled, too, and turned to walk away, but he grabbed her hand. "How about you?" He nodded. Ann gave his hand a quick squeeze. "There's somebody I want you to meet, Ma." He squeezed back. "Somebody special." He pushed the speaker button and put the receiver on the hook. "Ma, this is Ann."

"Merry Christmas, Ann," said a woman's voice. "How's the weather where you are?"

"It's beautiful." Neither her words nor her smile had anything to do with the weather.

"It's snowing like crazy here."

"It's snowing like crazy here, too, Ma. We're in South Dakota."

"South Dakota! That's right next door. Why didn't you bring Ann home for Christmas, Zachary?"

"Because it's been snowing like crazy here for…" He laughed. "I don't know. I lost track. But Ann's right. The weather's beautiful."

"Well, isn't *that* special," Hilda Beaudry teased. "If you two are as giddy as you sound, I'm guessing any kind of weather would be just fine with you. Is this my Christmas present?"

"All you want is a call, Ma. That's what you always tell me."

"I'm talking about Ann."

"Oh, no." Zach lifted his arm over Ann's head and draped it around her shoulders. "She's mine."

"Sam," Ma called out, "it's your brother!"

"Hey, Shortstop. How the hell are you? *Where* the hell are you?"

"He's in South Dakota," Ma said. Damn, she sounded excited. "Tell him, Zachary."

"I'm alive and well and crazy in love."

"She's on the phone with him, Sam."

"Yeah, be careful what you say," Zach warned cheerfully. Too cheerfully. He dialed it back, his smile fading. "I'm sorry I missed the wedding."

"Then get your sorry ass out here for New Year's. I've got a wife and kids to show off. And you've got…"

"Ann Drexler, Sam. I've heard a lot about you."

"Drexler? Are you the Drexler who runs the wild horse sanctuary I was just reading about?"

"My sister and I."

"Two sisters, yeah. Zach, you're with Wild Horse Annie and Mustang Sally?"

Zach did a double take. "Are you Wild Horse Annie?"

"There was an article in a magazine…" She redirected to the phone speaker. "That was months ago."

"I'm behind in my reading," Sam said.

"He's been a little busy," Ma put in.

"But I saw this article, and I was thinking… This is amazing, Zach. I was thinking of getting in touch with these ladies. Can you believe it?"

"This is Sam the Man," Zach explained to Ann. "He's got superpowers."

"I've got some money I need to get rid of, too. The article says Wild Horse Annie takes in wild horses. That's a cause I'd like to support."

"That would be lovely," Ann said.

"Good. Because we came into a ridiculous pile of money…"

"I haven't told her about that yet, Sam." He glanced at Ann. "He won the lottery."

"My daughter did, actually. Inherited the ticket from her mother. Long story. Did you know the most fun you can have with money is giving it away?"

"Sam the Man." Zach was grinning. Why had it taken him so long to make this call?

"So how do we get together?"

"I'm in need of a Best Man. I'm hoping for my big brother."

Silence.

Zach stared at the phone speaker.

"Sam?"

"Ma's cryin' on my shoulder here. You got it, Zach. Anytime, anywhere."

The rest of the conversation was mostly between the women. Crying begat crying, and Zach had to back away. The way he was feeling, he couldn't very well join in or he'd embarrass himself.

But when the phone was turned off, he turned the desk lamp off, too.

And he took Ann in his arms and held her in the dark. Not that he was crying. Cowboys didn't cry. His face was a little damp, but he'd been sweating that call for a while now. He meant to explain that to Ann when she kissed him—first one cheek, and then the other. But he kissed her sweet mouth instead. Sweet with the taste of her love, salty with the taste of his joy.

And warm with the promise that he would no longer be going down the road alone.

* * *

'THIS EVENING I'm flying to New York for two weeks,' Jasim imparted with a casualness that made her heart sink like a stone. 'That's why I had you brought here. I own this apartment and you'll be comfortable here while I'm abroad.'

'I can afford my own accommodation although I may not need it for long. I'll have another job by the time you get back—'

Jasim released a slightly harsh laugh. 'There's no need for you to look for another position. How would I ever see you? Don't you understand what I'm offering you?'

Elinor stood very still. 'No, I must be incredibly thick because I haven't quite worked out yet what you're offering me....'

His charismatic smile slashed his lean dark visage. 'Naturally, I want to take care of you....'

HPEX0110A

'No, thanks.' Elinor forced a smile and mentally willed him not to demean her with some sordid proposition. 'The only man who will ever take *care* of me with my agreement will be my husband. I'm willing to wait for you to come back but I'm not willing to be kept by you. I'm a very independent woman and what I give, I give freely.'

Jasim frowned. 'You make it all sound so serious.'

'What happened between us last night left pure chaos in its wake. Right now, I don't know whether I'm on my head or my heels. I'll stay for a while because I have nowhere else to go in the short term. So maybe it's good that you'll be away for a while.'

Jasim pulled out his wallet to extract a card. 'My private number,' he told her, presenting her with it as though it was a precious gift, which indeed it was. Many women would have done just about anything to gain access to that direct hotline to him, but his staff guarded his privacy with scrupulous care.

Before he could close the wallet, his blood ran cold in his veins. How could he have made such a serious oversight? What if he had got her pregnant? He knew that an unplanned pregnancy would engulf his life like an avalanche, crush his freedom and suffocate him. He barely stilled a shudder at the threat of such an outcome and thought how ironic it was that what his older brother had longed and prayed for to secure the line to the throne should strike Jasim as an absolute disaster....

* * *

What will proud Prince Jasim do if Elinor is expecting his royal baby? Perhaps an arranged marriage is the only solution! But will Elinor agree? Find out in DESERT PRINCE, BRIDE OF INNOCENCE by Lynne Graham [#2884], available from Harlequin Presents® in January 2010.

HPEX0110B

HARLEQUIN *Presents*

Bestselling Harlequin Presents author

Lynne Graham

brings you an exciting new miniseries:

PREGNANT BRIDES

Inexperienced and expecting, they're forced to marry

Collect them all:

DESERT PRINCE, BRIDE OF INNOCENCE

January 2010

RUTHLESS MAGNATE, CONVENIENT WIFE

February 2010

GREEK TYCOON, INEXPERIENCED MISTRESS

March 2010

HARLEQUIN® *Blaze*™

New Year, New Man!

*For the perfect New Year's punch,
blend the following:*

- *One woman determined to find her inner vixen*
- *A notorious—and notoriously hot!—playboy*
- *A provocative New Year's Eve bash*
- *An impulsive kiss that leads to a night of
explosive passion!*

When the clock hits midnight Claire Daniels
kisses the guy standing closest to her, but
the kiss doesn't end after the bells stop ringing….

Look for

Moonstruck

by *USA TODAY* bestselling author

JULIE KENNER

Available January

---

red-hot reads

REQUEST YOUR FREE BOOKS!

2 FREE NOVELS PLUS 2 FREE GIFTS!

SPECIAL EDITION®

Life, Love and Family!

YES! Please send me 2 FREE Silhouette Special Edition® novels and my 2 FREE gifts (gifts are worth about $10). After receiving them, if I don't wish to receive any more books, I can return the shipping statement marked "cancel." If I don't cancel, I will receive 6 brand-new novels every month and be billed just $4.24 per book in the U.S. or $4.99 per book in Canada. That's a savings of at least 15% off the cover price! It's quite a bargain! Shipping and handling is just 50¢ per book.* I understand that accepting the 2 free books and gifts places me under no obligation to buy anything. I can always return a shipment and cancel at any time. Even if I never buy another book from Silhouette, the two free books and gifts are mine to keep forever.

235 SDN EYN4 335 SDN EYPG

Name	(PLEASE PRINT)	
Address		Apt. #
City	State/Prov.	Zip/Postal Code

Signature (if under 18, a parent or guardian must sign)

Mail to the **Silhouette Reader Service:**
IN U.S.A.: P.O. Box 1867, Buffalo, NY 14240-1867
IN CANADA: P.O. Box 609, Fort Erie, Ontario L2A 5X3

Not valid to current subscribers of Silhouette Special Edition books.

Want to try two free books from another line?
Call 1-800-873-8635 or visit www.morefreebooks.com.

* Terms and prices subject to change without notice. Prices do not include applicable taxes. Sales tax applicable in N.Y. Canadian residents will be charged applicable provincial taxes and GST. Offer not valid in Quebec. This offer is limited to one order per household. All orders subject to approval. Credit or debit balances in a customer's account(s) may be offset by any other outstanding balance owed by or to the customer. Please allow 4 to 6 weeks for delivery. Offer available while quantities last.

Your Privacy: Silhouette is committed to protecting your privacy. Our Privacy Policy is available online at www.eHarlequin.com or upon request from the Reader Service. From time to time we make our lists of customers available to reputable third parties who may have a product or service of interest to you. If you would prefer we not share your name and address, please check here. ☐

SSE09R

COMING NEXT MONTH

Available December 29, 2009

#2017 PRESCRIPTION FOR ROMANCE—Marie Ferrarella
The Baby Chase

Dr. Paul Armstrong had a funny feeling about Ramona Tate, the beautiful new PR manager for his famous fertility clinic. Was she a spy trying to uncover the institute's secrets…or a well-intentioned ingenue trying to steal his very heart?

#2018 BRANDED WITH HIS BABY—Stella Bagwell
Men of the West

Private nurse Maura Donovan had sworn off men—until she was trapped in close quarters during a freak thunderstorm with her patient's irresistible grandson Quint Cantrell. One thing led to another, and now she was pregnant with the rich rancher's baby!

#2019 LOVE AND THE SINGLE DAD—Susan Crosby
The McCoys of Chance City

On a rare visit to his hometown, photojournalist Donovan McCoy discovered he was the father of a young son. But the newly minted single dad wouldn't be single for long, if family law attorney—and former Chance City beauty queen—Laura Bannister had anything to say about it.

#2020 THE BACHELOR'S NORTHBRIDGE BRIDE—Victoria Pade
Northbridge Nuptials

Prim redhead Kate Perry knew thrill seeker Ry Grayson spelled trouble. It was a case of the unstoppable bachelor colliding with the unmovable bachelorette. But did the undeniable attraction between them suggest there were some Northbridge Nuptials in their near future?

#2021 THE ENGAGEMENT PROJECT—Brenda Harlen
Brides & Babies

Gage Richmond was a love-'em-and-leave-'em type—until his CEO dad demanded he settle down or miss out on a promotion. Now it was time to see if beautiful research scientist Megan Rourke would pose as Gage's fake fiancée…and if their feelings would stay fake for long.

#2022 THE SHERIFF'S SECRET WIFE—Christyne Butler

Bartender Racy Dillon didn't expect to run into her hometown nemesis, Sheriff Gage Steele, in Vegas—let alone marry him in a moment of abandon! Now they were headed back to their small town with a big secret…but was there more to this whiplash wedding than met the eye?

SSECNMBPA1209